ANDREW STRONG

SCHOLASTIC

First published in the UK in 2009 by Scholastic Children's Books
An imprint of Scholastic Ltd
Euston House, 24 Eversholt Street
London, NW1 1DB, UK
Registered office: Westfield Road, Southam, Warwickshire, CV47 0RA
SCHOLASTIC and associated logos are trademarks and/
or registered trademarks of Scholastic Inc.

ISBN 978 1 407 10473 7

A CIP catalogue record for this book
is available from the British Library.

Printed by CPI Bookmarque, Croydon, CR0 4TD.
Papers used by Scholastic Children's Books are
made from wood grown in sustainable forests.

1 3 5 7 9 10 8 6 4 2

www.scholastic.co.uk/zone

to Mary, Jake and Ellie

With thanks to:
Catherine Clarke (shrewd mole)
Jackie Head (badgering mole)
Elv Moody (the mole who didn't stop digging)
Kirsty Skidmore (mole with vision)
Zöe Duncan and Polly Nolan
(two very patient moles)
Sarah Taylor Fergusson (meticulous mole)
Colin Williams
Llanbister School staff and pupils past
and present
The Happy Union
(and the nobbled jury of picklers)

A Note about Croquet

Croquet (pronounced *crow–kay*) is often portrayed as a tame pastime for older people. It is, however, a vicious, ruthless game.

Using a mallet about the size of a golf club, players take it in turns to hit a grapefruit-sized wooden ball through a series of hoops.

The game gets serious when one player's ball hits another's. This is called a "croquet". A croquet allows an extra turn, which can be used to send the opponent's ball whizzing across the grass into the flower beds, hedge, fish pond, etc.

ONE

A man with half a beard came thundering down the hotel staircase clutching a bare razor, shouting at the top of his voice. He wore just a towel and a face that suggested he wanted to murder someone.

"Who is the idiot in charge here?" he yelled.

"That would be my father," said Alf Picton, and pointed to the reception desk.

His father was nowhere to be seen, and Alf knew he was probably hiding away in his tiny workshop at the back of the Old Forge Hotel.

Alf picked up the little bell and rang it. "He should be along shortly," he said. Alf looked at the clock above the staircase. Thirty seconds was enough for his father to put down what he was doing. In thirty seconds he would ring the bell again.

After twenty-seven seconds a young woman with her hair full of soapsuds appeared at the bottom of the stairs. She marched across to the desk and stood beside the man with half a beard.

"This is just not good enough!" she cried. "What has happened to the water?"

A white-haired woman in a dressing gown joined them. A mouse dangled from her fingers.

"This place is infested with vermin!" she announced. "I've just found this in my bath."

Tom Picton emerged from his workshop and stood nodding his head. "I'm sorry, sir, madam," he said calmly. "I will attend to everything as soon as I can." He was clutching the skeleton of a violin, an antique instrument he was attempting to restore.

"Looks like you've got plenty of time to fix that guitar," said the man with half a beard.

"It's a fiddle," said the woman with soapy hair.

"I agree," said the man with half a beard. "Shall we demand a refund?"

"Alf," said his father, pointing towards the old lady. "Would you be so kind as to ask your sister to dispose of the deceased?"

Alf took the drowned mouse from the woman's fingers.

The man with the half beard and the woman with the shampoo hair stared at Alf's moth-bitten bellboy uniform. The faded, light blue material was stained, the cuffs and collar fraying. Here and there an unruly curl of his sandy hair pushed out from under the round hat perched at an angle on his head.

"This place is disgraceful," said the man with half a beard.

Alf's father shrugged.

"It's a complete dump," said the woman with soapsuds in her hair.

Alf's father nodded, as if he was agreeing with them.

"You should be ashamed of yourselves," said the white-haired woman in the dressing gown.

"We are," said Tom Picton.

"We're leaving!" they announced at the same time.

Alf couldn't let this happen. There were bills to pay, even if he had hidden most of them in the hedge. No more guests could be allowed to leave. He touched the edge of his tatty bellboy hat in salute and scurried off towards the kitchen, the mouse wrapped in his fingers.

Alf's sister, Hattie, was standing next to the dishwasher, frozen to the spot, clutching a bread knife, the blade pointing into the air. Alf looked back to realize the kitchen door had not closed behind him. The guests were still staring, but this time they seemed more interested in Hattie than in him.

"There!" Hattie yelled, directing her brother's alert green eyes to the wall opposite.

Up on a high shelf, perched on an ancient,

rusting tin marked "cake decorations", a big black crow peered down at them. Its beady stare was as full of contempt as the guests in reception.

"That's for you," said Alf, passing his sister the mouse. Hattie looked at the dead animal and sighed.

"Please, Alf," she said. "Do something about the bird."

Alf picked up a tea towel, and with one graceful flick, threw it over the crow. Then he jumped up on a chair and grabbed the creature.

"Cardew!" came a voice from outside. The back door from the garden opened and the hotel's oldest guest, Lord Craddock, stepped into the kitchen. "Where's that mad chef, Cardew?" said Lord Craddock. "He was supposed to bring me my coffee!"

"He's on the roof, sir," said Alf.

"What?" said Lord Craddock, his mouth hanging open under his white moustache. "Again?"

Whenever anyone insulted his cooking, the hotel chef climbed up on to the hotel roof and stayed there sulking, sometimes for days on end.

"He's been up there since breakfast," said Alf. "Someone complained that their egg was too runny."

Lord Craddock's eyes swivelled to the towel in Alf's hands. It was jumping about violently.

"Is that lunch under there?" asked the old man, noticing that Hattie brandished a knife in one hand and held a dead mouse in the other. "Can't we just have roast beef?" he said, looking a little concerned but not particularly surprised. "I hate foreign food."

"I'll get your coffee organized, sir," said Alf.

"Good boy, good boy," said Lord Craddock. "If I still had a regiment, you'd be marked out as officer material."

Alf released the bird from the back door, and then grabbed the kettle. He turned on the tap but nothing happened. "No water," he said, shaking his head in disbelief. He had forgotten about the dispute the man with half a beard and the woman with the soapsuds were having with his father.

His sister stood watching him, still clutching the dead mouse. "Time me, Hattie," Alf said, pushing his watch into her empty hand.

He raced through reception, past the desk, up the stairs, along the landing, then took another staircase up to the damp air of the unoccupied second floor. He pulled open a narrow door and squeezed along dark shelves of mouldering bed linen to the steep steps that led to the loft. Alf pushed his hand into the dark opening above his head and found the switch. A naked bulb came on, then began flickering wildly. He heard it fizz and expected it to pop at any moment.

Alf climbed up, then moved carefully through stacks of dusty magazines and old suitcases until he came to the water tank. It was empty. Either the pump had jammed or something was blocked. He stood back for a moment to examine the plumbing, then kicked the largest of the copper pipes. He heard a gurgle, a splutter, and the tank began to fill.

Grinning, he moved back the way he had come, switched off the light, closed the narrow door and bounded down the stairs. He swung around the banisters on the first floor and thumped straight into the man with half a beard. The two women were following him up the stairs to their rooms.

"Why don't you look where you are going?" the man snarled.

"Sorry," Alf gasped. "But I fixed the water. It's on again. You don't have to go now!"

The man's face twisted in mockery.

"Listen, boy, this hotel is dangerous. If the chef hasn't poisoned us already, he might fall off the roof and kill us. Perhaps the screaming, knife-wielding maniac in the kitchen will come after us. Or will we be electrocuted by the faulty wiring, or eaten alive by mice?"

Alf smiled weakly. He didn't know what to say. He slipped past them and headed back to the kitchen to fill the kettle.

"Three minutes and a bit," Hattie said, passing him the watch. She held out the dead mouse. "Poor thing," she sniffed. "Let's give it a decent funeral."

"Good idea," said Alf. "Three more guests are about to leave. We need something to cheer us up."

TWO

Alf followed Hattie into the garden, carrying a tray of coffee for Lord Craddock.

The old man had been playing his morning game of croquet with Purvis, the gardener, and was now seated on the terrace, banging his huge fist on the wrought-iron table.

"Croquet is a game for gentlemen," shouted Lord Craddock, his pipe clenched between his teeth. "It is essential you stick to the rules. Next time you take an extra turn, it will be a court martial!"

"I wasn't cheating, sir," said the gardener, putting on his gloves. "Yesterday you said it was perfectly fair to hit your opponent's ball into the hedge." Purvis never lost his temper. His face was leathery, weathered and patient.

"Nonsense!" boomed Lord Craddock, thumping the table again.

"I should be getting back to work," said Purvis. "Mr and Mrs Picton don't pay me to entertain you."

"Well, they should!" yelled the old man. "I am their most esteemed guest."

Alf placed the coffee carefully next to Lord Craddock. He muttered a thank you.

"Anything else I can get for you, sir?" Alf asked.

"Just a rifle." Lord Craddock winked. "So I can shoot that cheat." He pointed his upturned pipe at the gardener and made the sound of a gunshot. "Isn't it a beautiful day?" he continued. "Purvis may be a scoundrel, but he knows his business. The garden looks glorious."

Alf looked out over the lawns and vegetable beds to the meadows and hills beyond.

"Oh yes, sir," said Alf. "Best gardens and best views in all Milton Wells."

"Well, it's just a shame so very few people seem to realize that!" boomed the old man.

Alf headed on to meet Hattie in her little cemetery. It lay in the far corner of the garden, across the lawns, behind the apple trees and next to the old shed. Tiny creatures were buried there in neat rows in graves marked with small rectangles of slate. It was a sombre but peaceful haven in the ugly world of disgruntled guests.

Buried here were Finney, Hattie's goldfish, the slugs and snails Purvis had disposed of in a bucket of water, a frog Cardew the chef had stamped on in a rage and a thrush that had lost its way and flown into the French doors.

Hattie had finished digging a small hole for the drowned mouse and was laying it to rest. She smoothed over the soil, then took a neat piece of slate from a pile under the laurel hedge.

With a small stone she scratched the words UNKNOWN MOUSE on to the slate and stuck it into the earth.

"Would you like me to sound the Last Post?" Alf asked.

"Please," said his sister, standing up and bowing her head. Alf put his fist to his mouth and pretended he was a bugler. Hattie saluted. "He was a fine mouse," she said. "And didn't deserve to end up in that miserable old woman's bathwater."

Alf left Hattie to tidy up the cemetery and returned to his post in reception. To his surprise a tall, elegant woman with a neat suitcase in one hand and a briefcase in the other stood there. Alf noticed her long eyelashes. Her black hair was pulled off her face so tightly her skin seemed to stretch. Alf thought of pharaohs, for some reason. Of tombs, and pyramids. The woman looked down at Alf and inhaled deeply, as if holding on to impatience.

"Am I late?" she said.

"For what?" Alf asked.

"The Battle of Hastings," she said. "Has it started?"

"All over," said Alf. "About a thousand years ago."

"Is that a joke?" she snapped.

"I think you're in the wrong hotel, madam," said Alf at last, moving towards the door and opening it. "You must be looking for the Historians' Convention. You need the Imperial Hotel." He gestured towards the building across the town square. "Would you like me to carry your bags across?"

The woman paused for a moment, then smiled.

"Thank you," she said.

She held out the cases, and Alf took them, bowing slightly, then moved towards the door. He backed into it, holding it open for her, and she followed.

Alf glanced down at a label on the suitcase. He managed to read the name. Professor Helena Carmichael.

They crossed the square, weaving along the narrow paths between clipped shrubs, past the quartet of long benches surrounding the statue.

Professor Carmichael stopped, and peered up at the figure on the plinth. "Saint Barlow, isn't it?"

she said. "The founder of Milton Wells. What do you know about him?"

"Nothing," said Alf. "Probably came here when it was a just bare hill, lived in a stone hut and kept goats."

"Yes," laughed the professor, "yes, he probably did."

Alf was impressed. He thought no one outside of Milton Wells would have known the name of their saint.

When they reached the steps of the Imperial, Norman Jobson, the doorman, was there to meet them.

"Another customer fleeing?" said Jobson, grinning widely and showing off his white teeth. He grabbed the bags from Alf's hands.

"Fleeing?" said the professor. "I don't understand. Have I missed the conference?"

"Just started, madam," said Jobson. "Please follow me."

"One moment," said the professor. She took a step towards Alf and took her purse from a bag. "Thank you," she said, pushing a coin into his hand.

A tip. He hadn't been given a tip for at least a month. It would go into the old jug he kept in his room.

Alf stood at the bottom of the steps and looked

up at the bright reflections in the Imperial's great windows. Everything about the Imperial was perfect, even the doorman's teeth.

The glass reflected figures crossing the square from the Picton family's hotel. The man with half a beard and the young woman with shampoo in her hair were marching over, carrying suitcases.

Alf turned towards them. "May I be of assistance? Can I carry your. . .?"

"Don't touch anything of mine!" said the man with half a beard. "I'm lucky to get out of your hotel with my life."

"We're going to check into the Imperial," said the woman. "Perhaps they have the luxury of running water."

"And a chef who isn't insane," said the man.

Alf returned to the Old Forge Hotel to find the old woman who had discovered the mouse in her bath dragging her suitcases through reception.

"This place should be reduced to rubble!" she snapped. "Demolished before it falls down and kills everyone."

The door swung closed behind her.

Alf's father emerged from his hiding place. He had the ancient violin cradled in his arms. "I'm afraid things aren't looking good," he said. "Not good at all. A fine day like this and our guests are deserting us."

"It'll pick up," said Alf.

"Not unless there's a miracle," said his father. "And it better be soon."

"You haven't given up on the hotel, have you, Dad?" Alf asked him.

His father looked down at the violin and plucked at a string. "It's not that I've given up on the hotel," he said. "I think the hotel has given up on us."

THREE

Alf loved the hotel's routines. Eggs from the hen house, vegetables from the garden and the greenhouse, a delivery of groceries waiting to be collected from Blake's on North Parade. He cleaned shoes, helped prepare breakfast. Now and then he welcomed guests and showed them to their rooms. He usually had a much longer list of repairs and relished completing them before preparations for the evening meal began.

He enjoyed timing himself on his most prized possession, his grandfather's old silver fob watch, and finishing each task as quickly as possible.

Recently, however, he had had very little to do.

The potholers appeared. They were three men in red oversuits who set off every morning with bright faces full of enthusiasm and returned in the evening, exhausted but elated.

"Going far today?" Alf asked them.

"Don't need to go far," said one of them. "There are enough holes around here for a lifetime. Mill Hole Pot is just a stone's throw away."

"But we're going down Whittle Pot today," said the tallest one. "It's a tricky one. Quite a challenge."

"The easy pots are too busy," said the third. "We like the quieter, difficult caves."

One of them held out a big hand and dropped three coins into Alf's palm. Alf smiled. Three more for his tip jug.

They set off, marching silently in a line out of the hotel, their backpacks rattling with kit.

His father called him into the office. This was a narrow room behind the reception area with an old desk that looked like a dog had chewed it, and a grimy swivel chair stained with blotches of ink. A single fluorescent tube ran along the ceiling, but it was faulty, and hummed noisily. A calendar hung on the door that led to the workshop. It boasted scenes of Milton Wells; this month's was a view of the Chinese takeaway.

Alf's father placed a cardboard box on the desk and opened it up.

"I don't want Hattie to see these," he said. "But it has to be done."

"What?" Alf peered in. He saw a clutter of sinister metal contraptions. They had thick springs and rows of menacing triangular teeth. "What are they?"

"Mousetraps," said Dad. "Any more mice in

the hotel, we'll have the hygiene police in."

"You want me to set them?"

"Yes, everywhere you can. In empty rooms, cupboards in the kitchen."

"Hattie will hate me," said Alf.

"She won't know."

Alf didn't want to do it. He took a step away from the desk and folded his arms.

"Please," said Dad. "We'll be reported. What happens then? One mouse dropping, the hotel will be closed. It's them or us."

"All right," Alf sighed. "But don't tell Hattie. You know what she's like. She gets upset when Purvis sprays the greenfly on the cabbages."

"I thought she loved funerals," said Dad.

"Funerals, gravestones, yes, but that's because she feels sorry for the little creatures she buries. She wouldn't speak to me again if she knew I was doing this."

"Strange girl," said Dad. "Now go on, get on with it. I have to find some way of paying the milk bandits. The prices the dairy charges us, we might as well get our own cow."

There were twenty mousetraps: steel jaws that Alf pinched open and which snapped violently when a tiny metal tongue was triggered. Each needed to be loaded with a raisin and pushed into a hiding place.

He placed the old watch on the desk in reception. Off he went.

He put one trap behind the filing cabinet in the office, two at the back of kitchen cupboards, one in the mop cupboard, one in the laundry room. One went under the stairs, one under each of the two sofas in the lounge. He unlocked the door to the ballroom, and kicked it when it wouldn't open.

He hated the ballroom; it was dark and empty and hadn't been used for years. He set one trap in a dusty, bare corner, one under a cold cast-iron radiator, another in the filthy old fireplace. Then he put two in each of the three biggest unoccupied rooms on the first floor.

He felt like an executioner, someone who would have the blood of innocent creatures on his hands. He wouldn't do it to a dog or a cat. Why a mouse? He thought this as he set each one, and each time he would hear his father's words: *It's them or us*, and he knew that's how it was.

As he was placing the last trap he heard his mother call and realized she was home from her Saturday job at the supermarket. Sarah Picton spent the weekdays at the college in Wornham, training to be an accountant. She was always on the go.

"Alf," she shouted, "we need you!" She was standing at the foot of the stairs with a grave look on her face. "Crisis meeting," she said.

He raced downstairs and swept up his watch. Six minutes thirty-three seconds.

The family gathered in the hotel lounge, a room in which guests once relaxed with coffee, rustled newspapers or sat quietly and read. But the sofas and armchairs hadn't been used since Christmas. The view from one end of the room was of the hotel gardens and the hills beyond. At the opposite end the room looked out over the great plane trees around Saint Barlow Square.

Alf opened the windows and saw Purvis busy pushing the old mower across the lawn. Lord Craddock was walking behind him, waving his pipe in the air.

"We used gliders!" Alf could hear Craddock shouting over the mower. "Silently, they floated across the fields and. . ."

"Right," said Alf's dad, dropping into the sofa and squaring a pile of loose papers on his knees. "I've been going through a few things and have made a decision."

Alf's mother was holding a mug of tea and eating a sandwich.

"It better be good," she said.

"Very good," added Hattie.

Tom Picton beckoned them all to sit down around him.

"We are in a mess," he announced.

"Really?" said Mum, raising her eyebrows in mock surprise.

"There are just six guests here. We have twenty-four rooms. Max and Tilda are only here because their house has still not been fully refurbished since the flood, there are the potholers, who only stay for a few days before joining their mates on the campsite, and, of course, Lord Craddock."

"Who has been here for years, Tom," said Mum, "and hasn't paid us a penny for at least the last five!"

"Let's not go through that again," said Dad.

"He's costing us a fortune."

"But he brings this place a bit of class, Sarah," said Dad. He turned to Alf and Hattie. "Your grandfather loved him. He thought he was a lucky mascot."

"Some luck," said Mum.

"I like him," said Hattie. "He's nice. He smells funny, but he's nice."

"His stories are good," said Alf. "He's lived through a lot."

"Yes, a true hero," said Dad. "A remarkable man."

"Yes, well. . ." said Mum. "I wish he wouldn't smoke that horrible pipe. Anyway. What are we going to do? What's the plan? May I remind you the hotel is no longer a business. It's a joke. Your father earns more money mending violins."

"Do you, Dad?" said Hattie, unsure whether this was good news.

"Your mother is right. I am making some money from repairing instruments. But the hotel isn't making any money at all. We owe a lot of people a lot of money. I'm surprised we don't get more bills than we do!"

Alf gulped, and felt himself go red in the face. Every morning he would ensure he intercepted the postman's delivery. Anything that looked like a bill he stuffed into the hedge.

Dad picked up the sheaf of papers on his lap. "These are details of houses in Wornham; your mum picked them up today. As things stand, we can sell the hotel, buy a small place, have some money to start again. And then you two can go back to school."

While they'd been needed in the hotel there was never any mention of going to school.

"What?" said Hattie and Alf at the same time.

"Yes. Sell up, move, start afresh," said their dad. "I'd like to make violins full time."

"You can't sell up," said Alf. "I love it here."

"It's home," said Hattie.

"We'll never find another place like this," said Alf.

"You're right there," his mother snapped.

"And what about Cardew and Purvis and Lord Craddock? What will they do?" asked Alf.

"Well, they'll have to move on, too," said Alf's dad.

"That's not fair," said Hattie.

"Cardew will never find another job," said Alf.

"He's useless," said Hattie.

"And where will Lord Craddock live?" cried Alf. "Please, Dad. There must be another way!"

"Your father is right. There is no other way," said Mum. "We're broke. The longer we go on, the more money we owe. When I qualify as an accountant I'll earn ten times what we make here, even when things are going well."

From somewhere above them they heard a clatter of tiles, then a low rumble. There was a crack, and a large shadow fell past the window.

Alf crossed the room to look. He saw the chef scramble to his feet and limp off like a wounded fox. His watch told him it was a quarter to six. Cardew had been on the roof for nine hours and eight minutes.

A few moments later Cardew appeared in the doorway to the lounge. He was a short, plump man with a mess of black greasy hair. He looked permanently tired, unshaven and unhappy.

"Excuse me, Mr Picton," he said, his Welsh accent softer than usual, as if he was about to give them bad news. "I think I have broken my arm."

FOUR

Tom Picton wasn't overjoyed about the prospect of cooking. When he worked in the kitchen he liked to listen to music that wasn't particularly appreciated by his children. Today it was a mournful and ancient violin tune.

"It's the magnificent Billy Coleman," said Tom, "the greatest fiddler of all time."

"Sounds like it was recorded in a shed," said Hattie.

"That's because it was," said her father. "In a cowshed."

"I'd rather listen to the cow," said Hattie.

Alf laid the tables in the dim light of the old dining room. The curtains were kept drawn in the evenings and candles were lit to create what Cardew liked to call "the right mood". To Alf it made the place seem like a fairy-tale grotto. But when Cardew was cooking, it was a good thing guests couldn't see too much of what they were eating.

But now Cardew was at the hospital, Alf's father was in the kitchen.

The first course was soup made with tomatoes from the hotel greenhouse and onions from the vegetable garden. This was followed by something Tom Picton called "Old Forge Pie".

"It's a sort of mixture of things," he explained to his children. "The vegetarians like spicy food. Lord Craddock can't taste anything. So I'll make it spicy for them and make sure it has plenty of crunch for him. He likes crunchy onions, particularly."

Alf placed the meals before the quiet couple in the corner. They stared suspiciously at their food, and then at each other. Alf thought they looked like twins. Max had a small goatee beard, and Tilda had a tiny nose and pretty eyes. They both had long hair, parted in the middle, and always looked slightly disgruntled.

"Lovely soup," said Lord Craddock. "What was it? Mushroom?"

In the kitchen Alf watched his father throwing things into a mixing bowl. His eyes were closed and the music was even louder.

"Shouldn't you look at what you're doing?" suggested Alf.

"I am an artist," Dad answered, breaking an egg

into the bowl, then grating some lemon. "I don't look, I feel!"

"Yes, but can you cook?" asked Hattie, scowling.

They heard footsteps coming through reception, then Sarah Picton appeared, took off her coat, slung it down and filled the kettle.

"It looks like you're cooking for a while yet, Tom," she said. "Cardew will be in plaster for at least a month."

"This place!" Alf's father sighed. "It's cursed."

"Come on," said Alf. "Let's eat."

When the guests had finished their meals, Alf led the family through to the dining room and lit a candle. They didn't often sit down together. His mum always ate on the move, Hattie liked picnicking in her cemetery, and Dad spent every spare moment in his workshop.

When his parents were eating, and Alf sensed they were a little calmer, he decided to return to the subject of the hotel.

"We're not really going to leave, are we?" he asked.

His father put down his fork and took a sip of water. "Alf, I'm sorry. I love this old place as much as you. But we can't go on."

"I'm not going anywhere else," said Alf, firmly.

28

"What?" Dad was a little taken aback. "Alf, I don't think you. . ."

"Give us more time," Alf said. "Let's say three months. Hattie and I will think of something. We'll save this place."

"We can't go on that long," said Mum. "The hotel needs too much money spent on it. Money we don't have. We have too many bills, and not enough guests. It's as simple as that. We can sell up, buy somewhere small to live, start again. I'm sorry."

"No," said Hattie, holding back tears. "I won't go."

"The hotel has been in the family for a long, long time," said Dad. "And as much as I want to stay here, it isn't possible. It has to go up for sale immediately."

"No, no, no," said Alf. "You have to give us a chance. That's not fair. This is everything to us. It's all we've ever known."

Tom Picton sighed and closed his eyes. "It's all I've ever known too. I don't want to do this either, Alf," he said. "But it's all over. We have to sell."

"Dad," said Hattie, her eyes full of tears. "Don't sell. Please. Where will we go?"

"There are some nice houses in Wornham," said Mum.

"Wornham's horrible!" said Alf.

"Your father has decided," said Mum. "And that's that."

"You should give us a chance," said Alf. "Just a few more months to come up with something."

"Please, Dad," said Hattie.

Tom Picton sat back and folded his arms. Alf could see he was weakening.

"You know the game's up, Tom," said Mum. "Don't be soft. Put it up for sale now."

"Mum!" cried Hattie. "You really want to go, don't you?"

"Hattie, darling, it's business," she answered. "We might as well just throw money away. We need to be tough, take tough decisions."

"Give us one last chance," said Alf. "We'll think of something, won't we, Hattie?"

"Don't build up your hopes, please," said Mum. "If we could make a go of it here, we would. I want to put it up for sale immediately. Tom, what do you say?"

"We're selling up," he said. "But selling a business like this won't happen overnight. So, I'll lay down a challenge to you both. Why not see if you can fill this place for, let's say, three nights. You'll see how hard it is. If you can get guests in every single room for just three nights between now and the end of the month, you might convince me that the Old Forge isn't a sinking ship."

"And then you won't sell?" said Alf.

"You won't do it," said Dad.

FIVE

"Can you do any work with one arm in plaster, Cardew?" Tom Picton asked the unshaven Welshman, whose dark beard was beginning to make him look more grumpy and sinister.

"Well, unfortunately," said Cardew, "it is my right hand that is broke. I can use my left to do this and that," he explained vaguely, "but not much."

"Any ideas, Alf?" his father asked him.

Alf was preparing to polish shoes in the corner of the kitchen. He had lined up three pairs of Lord Craddock's shoes: an identical pair of brogues, one brown and one black, and a pair of boots the old man wore in the garden.

He lay his watch next to them and began timing.

"I think Cardew should help Purvis in the garden," said Alf, flicking open a tin of polish.

"You could hold a hose, couldn't you?" asked Dad.

"All right," said Cardew and scowled. "But don't blame me if I kill everything."

The brush zipped across Craddock's shoes, Alf's elbow just a blur. He switched from black to brown polish, and with a flourish produced a buffing rag to give the shine. He threw the tins and brushes back in their box and placed Lord Craddock's shoes on an old tray.

"Two minutes seven seconds," he said aloud to himself. He pushed through the door into the reception. Hattie was there, doodling at the desk, her head leaning on her hand. Alf bounded up the stairs.

Lord Craddock's room overlooked the back of the hotel. Alf placed the shoes next to the door and knocked. He heard Craddock yell, "Thank you!" from inside, then the door opened and the old man stood there, smartly dressed as usual, his unlit pipe gripped between his teeth. He studied Alf's face.

"The hotel's up against it, isn't it, old chap?" said Lord Craddock. "I saw the deserters sneaking off yesterday. Cowards, the lot of them."

Alf nodded. He didn't want to say too much, but he knew Lord Craddock could be trusted.

"Dad doesn't think we can carry on for much longer," he said.

Craddock nodded. He looked grim for a few seconds, then took the pipe from his mouth and stepped into the corridor. He looked left and right, then over Alf's head, down into the reception.

"This hotel will never, never surrender!" he whispered. He had a look of conviction in his eyes that somehow Alf trusted. "You and I will come up with something. Let's put our heads together. We must have a strategy if we're to save this place. And a good strategy means the considered deployment of resources, the mobilization of forces. Then tactics, details, all that sort of thing. Come in, come in."

The old man's room was the largest in the hotel, with three tall windows overlooking the garden. Craddock had been here so long it had become his own. Photos and memorabilia hung on the walls. Craddock's desk was set before the middle window, and in one corner, on a tall hat stand, were his military caps, a bowler and a glossy top hat.

"Everything I own is in here, dear boy," he said. "And as you probably know, money's a little thin on the ground, so, if you sell up, I'll be in a bit of a pickle. But as I said, it isn't going to happen."

Lord Craddock stood at the window and looked out over the garden, his giant hands clasped behind his back. Although he could no longer afford to pay for the room, he had kept his elegant suits. He stooped slightly but was still an imposing figure.

Alf watched the old man narrow his eyes and stare out into the distance. He was like a commander assessing the lie of the land.

"The very first thing we have to do is gather intelligence," said Lord Craddock. "You need to find your enemy's weakness. Sometimes it can be staring you in the face, so obvious you don't notice."

"Enemy?" said Alf. "Who's our enemy?"

Craddock spun around and stared at him. "What? The enemy? The Imperial Hotel, of course! Find their weakness, Alf, gather intelligence, then we'll find our strategy, muster our troops, resources, and then, my boy, and then. . ."

Alf saw his clear blue eyes become sharp, bright points of light.

"And then, we attack!"

Craddock stared at Alf for a few moments before adding, "I shall designate myself Field Marshall, and you will be my general. General Alf."

"What about Hattie?" said Alf, wondering if Craddock was getting a bit carried away.

"Hattie?" Lord Craddock looked as if he had just received a nasty shock. "A girl?"

"Yes, she's a girl," said Alf. "She'll have to be a general too, or she won't play."

"Play?" spluttered Craddock, raising his eyebrows as well as his voice. "This isn't play, this is war!"

"Both of us generals, please. General Alf and General Hattie."

"Right, all right." Craddock turned back to the window. "Your parents are excellent commanders in the field, brigadiers, both of them. And Purvis, he's a captain."

"What about Cardew?" said Alf.

"He's an idiot," said Craddock.

"He might be useful," said Alf. "He did climb on the roof, after all!"

"He's a useless clown," said Craddock. "A bearded buffoon!" The old man marched over to the hat stand in the corner and picked off his military cap. He placed it on his head.

"Were you a general?" asked Alf.

Craddock stood to attention and saluted. Alf noticed the size of the old man's hand – it looked too big for his body.

"Promise not to tell anyone," said the old man.

"Promise," said Alf.

"I worked underground." He winked. "Sabotage and all that. But that's between us, understand?"

Alf nodded.

"Now, you must get intelligence, Alf," said Craddock. "As soon as you can"

Alf saluted. "Yes, sir," he said, "General Lord Craddock, sir!"

SIX

"I'm frightened," said Hattie. "What happens if we have to leave here? Where do we go?"

"Never mind about that," said Alf. "Let's concentrate on the enemy for a while. Craddock says we need to get into the Imperial and discover their weakness. He thinks it's a war. We're generals now."

"I hate war," said Hattie. "I hate war and killing and things dying. It's not right."

Brother and sister sat on stools behind the reception desk, their chins set in their palms.

Alf was staring up at the framed photo of their great-grandfather, Albert, and his wife, Mary, standing on the steps of the Old Forge holding a large silver cup. It was the award for "Milton Wells' Hotel of the Year". It was the only year the hotel had ever won the accolade. The couple looked so proud, and were surrounded by a staff of almost twenty. It seemed unbelievable to Alf that there could have been so many people working in the Old Forge.

"How did Albert do it?" said Alf. "The Imperial has won the cup every other year before and since. What happened that one year?"

"I can't imagine the Old Forge ever getting more customers than the Imperial," said Hattie. "Look at this place. It isn't very smart, is it?"

Alf didn't want to admit it, but wherever he looked there was something not quite right. Wallpaper was peeling, the ceiling was cracked and stained, light fittings were slipping out of place, and electrical wires bulged dangerously. Although Alf was keen to have a go at fixing most things, his father would not allow him up a ladder. If Alf couldn't reach it, it didn't get fixed.

From the photograph, their great-grandfather looked down gravely at them. The hotel had been the family business for nearly a hundred years. Albert Picton would curse them if they gave up on the Old Forge.

"There must be a way to fight back," said Alf. "It can't be impossible. If Albert did it, then so can we."

"I'm with you!" said Hattie. "Of course I am! But what do we do?"

"We have to get into the Imperial somehow, see what their weakness is. Jobson won't let us up the steps, never mind in through the doors. How do we get past him?"

They sat silently for a few minutes, listening to the hotel's water pipes rattle, and the floorboards creaking above their heads.

"I've got it!" said Alf. "Professor Carmichael! Perhaps we could send her something."

"Who?" said Hattie.

"A woman who came in here thinking it was the Imperial. She was looking for the Battle of Hastings."

"Why is everyone so interested in fighting?" sighed Hattie.

The potholers came down the stairs.

"You two look bored out of your minds," said the first. "You should get outside."

"Fresh air," said the tall one. "A long walk. Open countryside. Meadows, flowers."

"Fancy a day potholing?" said the third. "Join the moldywarps!"

"What are moldywarps?" asked Hattie.

"We are! Potholers are known as moldywarps. It's a very old word that means mole. We're like moles, you see. We like tunnels. So are you coming with us?"

"No thanks," said Hattie. "Sounds horrible."

"I would," said Alf. "But I've got too much to do."

"It's a hard life," said the first. "Still, if you fancy a day out, ask your mum and dad if you can come with us. We'll show you the caves."

"I'd like that," said Alf, filling their flasks and handing them back.

"See you later!" the tall one winked, and the three adventurers set off.

"Flowers!" Alf exclaimed suddenly. "One of the potholers, Hattie. He just mentioned flowers! That's it!"

Hattie screwed up her face. "What are you talking about?"

"Come on, I'll explain in a minute. Let's find Purvis. He'll know the flowers we'll need!"

Alf and Hattie set off around the square, approaching the Imperial from a direction that wouldn't make it so obvious to Jobson the doorman who they were. Wearing wool hats and sunglasses, they looked like cat burglars and a little ridiculous in the bright sunshine.

But Alf carried a huge bouquet of flowers in front of his face, and Hattie a smaller one in front of hers. They could peer through the stalks to see where they were going, but it was unlikely anyone would recognize them.

"Purvis is a genius," said Hattie. "These are gorgeous."

"Now remember, we're gathering intelligence. Discover their weakness. They must have one."

"Bet they don't," said Hattie.

The flowers sprayed out of their arms in an explosion of colour. As they mounted the steps of the Imperial, Jobson stepped out.

"Can I help you?" he said.

"Delivery for Professor Carmichael," said Alf, disguising his voice as well as he could.

Jobson nodded and opened one of the large glass doors. Alf tried not to grin, but he couldn't help it. They were inside the Imperial. It was easy.

He admired the ornate ceilings and the sparkling chandeliers. As he passed through the reception he saw relaxed groups chatting on leather sofas, drinking coffee, a waiter taking an order, a waitress placing a plate of cakes upon a table.

He glanced over at Hattie. She simply shook her head, and Alf knew what this meant. They didn't stand a chance. They couldn't compete with the luxury and elegance of the Imperial Hotel.

Behind the long desk were three women, all seated, dressed in black. They looked organized, businesslike.

Alf shifted the bouquet from his face. "Flowers for Professor Helena Carmichael," he said.

"Well, she's a very lucky lady," said the receptionist, her glossed lips smiling broadly. She picked up a phone and seconds later a porter appeared. "Martin, would you take these flowers to Professor Carmichael in room two three six?" said the receptionist.

"Oh, that's all right," said Alf, "we'd like to present them ourselves."

"We are her nephew and niece," said Hattie. "We want it to be a surprise."

"I'll just check she's there," said the receptionist. She dismissed the porter with a nod, and picked up the phone. "Professor Carmichael, you have visitors. Shall I send them up?"

The receptionist put down the phone and smiled at the children. "Second floor," she said. "Room two three six."

"Thanks," said Alf, moving towards the stairs.

"What now?" said Hattie.

"I'll think of something," said Alf.

The corridor of the second floor was quiet; their feet made no sound as they trod the long carpet between the rooms.

"Here," said Alf. They stood outside her door, and knocked.

"My goodness," said the professor when she saw them standing there. "Are these for me? Please, come in." She took off her glasses and stood aside for them. Alf could see from the pile of papers on the desk by the window that she had been working.

The room looked out on to the square. The windows were open, and the professor's papers fluttered in the breeze.

"A present from the Old Forge Hotel," said Alf.

He and Hattie lay the two bouquets on the bed. Alf pulled off his sunglasses, and the professor recognized him.

"I don't understand," she said.

"Well," Alf began, "there's an old tradition: anyone who knows the name of our founding saint receives a bouquet."

"That's lovely!" said the professor. "But two bouquets?"

"Yes," Alf mumbled. "That's the tradition. Two bouquets." He glanced at the desk. "What are you working on?"

"Well, I was trying to write a book about something very dull," she explained. "But yesterday I discovered one of the great mysteries of Milton Wells. I'm quite intrigued by it. Have you ever heard of the Invisible Claw?"

Alf gasped. When he was very small, a guest had told him the story of a strange creature that was supposed to haunt the Imperial Hotel. Even now Alf felt a slight shiver when he heard those words.

"I had nightmares about the Invisible Claw when I was young."

"And I remember you frightening me with the story, too," said Hattie.

"But I didn't think it was true," added Alf.

The professor leaned forward as if she was about to share top-secret information. "The owners of the Imperial Hotel don't like people to know about it. But many years ago, long before I was born, the Imperial Hotel was even grander than it is today. Film stars, even royalty stayed here. One of its most illustrious guests was Ludwig, the king of Pomerania."

"The king of where?" said Hattie.

"It's a country that no longer exists," said the professor. "It was somewhere between Germany and Poland. The thing is," she continued, looking at them, "King Ludwig fled Pomerania when his people rose up against him. He came to England looking for somewhere to hide. He and his wife, Queen Henrietta, stayed at the Imperial. They even brought their crown jewels, and had them locked in the hotel safe."

"And the jewels disappeared?" said Alf.

"Indeed. And all that was found were mysterious, three-pronged claw marks in the wall of the hotel strongroom."

"Claw marks?" said Hattie. "From what sort of animal?"

"Well, that's part of the mystery. Who or what

made those marks was never discovered. But the jewels disappeared. King Ludwig blamed the hotel, but the managers claimed they were completely innocent."

"Didn't the police find anything?" asked Alf.

"No, that's the thing," said the professor. "The country's best detectives were called. The place was searched high and low. Nothing. The thief was never discovered. The only clue, those strange marks."

"The Invisible Claw," said Alf.

"Was this a long time ago?" asked Hattie.

"Sixty years or so," said the professor.

"Then the Invisible Claw is probably dead now," said Hattie.

"Well, yes, but it's still an exciting story, and it would make a thrilling book," said the professor. "But the hotel, to this day, is embarrassed by what happened. They still try to keep it quiet."

"Do you like this hotel, Professor?" Alf asked.

"Yes, it's very nice. We come here every year, the historians."

"Why would anyone stay anywhere else?" said Alf bitterly.

The professor folded her arms. "What's the name of your hotel?"

"The Old Forge," they answered together.

"And is everything all right there?"

Alf looked at his sister.

"Fine. Except everything keeps dying," said Hattie. "You better put those flowers in water soon."

"Well, we won't keep you," said Alf, gloomily.

"And thank you for the flowers," said the professor. "I'm here for a few days yet." She stood up and walked towards the door. "I hope we bump into each other again," she said.

Alf and Hattie strolled out through the main doors of the Imperial, which had been left open to allow cool air to drift into the reception.

Alf noticed Jobson, his face almost the same bright red as his jacket, standing in the shadow of a tree set in the pavement, talking with two middle-aged men. Alf could see the men weren't very happy about something.

"It's just not something we do," said Jobson, calmly.

"Well, you should think about it, on a day like this," said one of the men, waving a hand towards the square. "It's so stuffy inside. If the hotel had a shed with a few deckchairs in it, then we could make use of the square. There's nowhere else to sit."

Alf looked over towards the statue of Saint Barlow.

"What do you notice, Hattie?" he said.

"Nothing," said Hattie. "Old people. Being boring."

"Around the statue," said Alf.

"People on benches. Lots of them. Shading from the sun. There's nothing else to do. It's Sunday in Milton Wells."

"Exactly," said Alf. "I think we've found the answer. I think I know the Imperial Hotel's one weakness."

"That it doesn't have deckchairs?" said Hattie.

"No," said Alf. "The Imperial doesn't have a garden. We do, and it's easily the best in Milton Wells. We just have to make sure everyone here gets to know about it."

SEVEN

Alf discovered his father on the first floor heaving a wardrobe along the landing. It looked like someone was moving house.

"Max and Tilda have asked your mother if they can have an extra room," he puffed. "They want it empty of furniture and want to decorate it completely white. Mum thinks we should let them." He leant on an old dressing table for a second. "Not that it matters what we think. They've started in there already."

"Painting it white? What for?" asked Alf.

"A place for them to meditate," said Dad. "And Mum thinks meditation will help her concentrate. That's what Max has told her. I expect they'll be shut up in there all day redecorating."

Alf helped his father move the rest of the unwanted furniture, then followed him downstairs.

"So the hotel will become like a temple?" Alf asked. "People with their eyes closed, chanting, that sort of stuff?"

"More like a temple of doom!" Dad laughed. "Anyway, lunch is on now. Are you hungry? Only Craddock to serve, though."

"So can I tell you about the Imperial?" said Alf, pleading. He trailed behind his father into the kitchen.

"Sausages and mash," said Dad, opening the fridge.

"Fine," said Alf. "And I think I know how we can win the war!"

"What?" said his father, taking a large frying pan down from a shelf.

"I think I know how to we can begin to fight back. Against the Imperial."

"Lay the table for Lord Craddock first. You're beginning to sound like him. And then go and tell him lunch will be a bit earlier today."

Alf realized his father was too distracted to listen. He set Lord Craddock's place, then went out to find him. The old man would be interested in what he had to say.

Craddock was sitting on the terrace, his pipe set between his teeth. He had his eyes closed and was humming. A rolled-up newspaper was clenched in one of his massive hands.

"Lord Craddock," whispered Alf.

"Yes, m'boy," said the old man without opening his eyes.

"Intelligence mission complete. I think I have discovered the Imperial's weakness."

Craddock's eyes opened. He sat up, suddenly excited.

"Excellent. What's the plan?"

"It's what you said. The answer is staring us in the face. The garden. The Imperial doesn't have a garden."

"Yes, go on," said Craddock.

"We got into the Imperial without much difficulty. Hid behind bouquets of flowers."

"Excellent camouflage," said Craddock, nodding.

"It's a smart place, sir. Grand piano, chandeliers, swimming pool. But no garden. And guests wanted to hire deckchairs but the Imperial won't do that. All the benches in the square were taken up. There was nowhere for anyone to sit and enjoy the sunshine. We have to make more of our garden, somehow."

Craddock nodded. "Good work," he said. But Alf could see he was also a little disappointed.

"Thing is," said Craddock after a while, "I don't think it's quite enough. We need something more." He tapped the rolled newspaper on the table. "We need to hit the Imperial hard. Artillery and all that."

On the far side of the garden, just inside a

long wall, where the greenhouses stood, Purvis was working on the vegetable plot. In the opposite corner, beyond the orchard, Hattie was crouching down. She looked like she was praying. It was a paradise here, and one Alf didn't want to lose.

The old man had closed his eyes again and seemed to be listening to a tune in his head, conducting it with the baton of rolled newspaper.

"The garden," Alf whispered to himself. "The secret lies here, somewhere."

"What?" said Craddock suddenly, glaring at him.

Alf took a step away from the old man. Lord Craddock seemed alarmed. His face had changed.

"What did you just say?" Craddock's voice was strained.

Alf swallowed hard. "I said the secret must be hidden here. That's all."

"What secret?" Craddock snapped. "What do you know?"

Alf shrunk back. Craddock's eyes narrowed. Alf noticed the old man's immense fingers gripping the edge of the table. His other hand pointed the tube of newspaper at Alf. Craddock was shaking and looked quite sinister.

"All I said was," Alf answered nervously, "the

garden is our secret weapon. It could save us. We need to think of some way of making the most of it."

Lord Craddock relaxed. "Only one thing this garden is good for," said the old man, calmer now. "And that's beating Purvis at croquet."

A wasp came out of nowhere and began doodling shapes in the air above the table.

Alf thought for a moment. "Do you know everything about croquet, Lord Craddock?"

"All there is to know, Alf. A game for gentlemen." He puffed on his pipe, watching the wasp carefully.

"Then that's what we'll do," said Alf.

"What?" said Craddock.

"We'll have a croquet afternoon. You can teach everyone the rules, can't you?"

Craddock's eyes lit up again. "And once we get them here, they'll see this view and. . ."

"And the Imperial won't stand a chance!" said Alf.

Hattie was making her way across the garden.

"That's a fine idea, Alf," said Lord Craddock. "And what better time to start than today!" The wasp made one last circuit above the old man's head before landing on the table. Alf watched it crawl across the surface, stopping to investigate a crumb of something.

"Lunch will be ready soon, sir," Alf remembered his father's message. "Nearly forgot to tell you."

"Excellent. I'm ravenous." Craddock's eyes were on the wasp.

Hattie stepped up on to the terrace.

"Good funeral?" Alf asked.

"I was just tidying up. No funerals today. Can't find anything dead."

Lord Craddock slammed down the newspaper. "Got it. There you are."

He held out the flattened wasp.

"I wish you hadn't done that," said Hattie, taking the dead insect carefully by the wing.

Lord Craddock stood up. "Always hit the enemy hard," he said. "And be utterly ruthless."

"And that's what we're going to do to the Imperial, Hattie," said Alf. "Hit them hard."

"With a newspaper?" asked Hattie, a little confused. She was staring at the wasp dangling from her fingers.

"No," Alf answered, laughing. "With croquet mallets!"

EIGHT

Straight after lunch, Alf made sure everything was ready. Purvis wanted the garden to look perfect. Hattie was making sandwiches, her father baking cakes. Cardew could use his one good hand to collect the entrance fee.

The square was even busier in the afternoon. The benches were full, people were sitting on walls, on the grass, some in the shade of the plain trees, others sunbathing. Alf had prepared a speech. He checked his watch, then strode out into the sunshine in his bellboy uniform, stood facing the statue of Saint Barlow, coughed and began.

"Ladies and gentleman. The Old Forge Hotel's croquet tournament begins at three o'clock." Alf felt eyes turning on him. "The well-known croquet expert Lord Craddock will referee the competition. Places are limited. The tournament will comprise a brief introduction to the game, including rules, followed by a knockout. Beginners are welcome. Entrance to the competition includes a delicious afternoon tea."

He had everyone's attention now; he could sense it. "First prize will be a free weekend at the tournament's venue, the Old Forge Hotel, just across the square."

"What a wonderful idea!" someone piped.

"A lovely thing to do on such an afternoon," said another.

"I've always wanted to play croquet," said a third voice.

Alf glanced across to the Imperial Hotel to see Norman Jobson staring at him. Alf was about to turn away when someone called his name.

It was Professor Carmichael.

"Hello again," she said.

"Hello," said Alf. "No lectures this afternoon?"

"Next one is this evening, a talk on the history of Milton Wells," she explained. "Do you know this little town goes back thousands of years?"

Alf shook his head. "So will you come to our croquet tournament?" he asked.

"Of course," the professor answered, "and I'll bring a few others too." She smiled, waved and turned away. Alf raced back to the hotel to report his good news.

*

In the garden Hattie was feeding a line of bunting up to her father, who was standing at the top of a stepladder. The tiny flags ran all the way around the competition area and fluttered merrily in the breeze.

"It's just a shame Mum thinks her white room is more important," said Hattie. "She should be here with us instead of redecorating."

"Well, you never know," said Dad, coming down the ladder, squinting as he looked up to admire the bunting. "Why not try everything? Croquet may appeal to some people, meditation to others. I just hope Max and Tilda aren't meditating and your mother's doing all the redecorating."

Craddock, dressed in a white suit and a straw hat, his hands gripped behind his back, inspected the preparations.

The lawns had been mowed to perfection. The croquet hoops were in position and the rack of brightly coloured mallets and balls placed at the far end.

Alf crossed the terrace. Below, on the other side of the garden by the side entrance, Cardew, his arm in a sling, held a book of tickets. He watched as Purvis set up a table for admission fees to be collected. The canny gardener had even arranged a sale of plants.

For the first time in many years, the dining room's French doors were open to the terrace. Tables just inside were laid with white tablecloths and Purvis had seen to it that each was decorated with a small bouquet. Plates of sandwiches and cakes had been placed on each table. Chairs had been brought out and placed along the terrace for spectators, or for competitors waiting to play. Alf was excited. Everything was ready.

"It looks perfect, doesn't it?" shouted Craddock. "Such a simple idea. But ingenious."

"I just hope they come," said Alf.

"They will, boy. You will have impressed them, I'm sure."

"Nothing can go wrong now, can it?" said Alf.

"Impossible!" Craddock shouted back.

Just before three o'clock the first competitors arrived, two women who explained they were guests at the Imperial, but not there for the conference.

"Good afternoon, ladies," said Lord Craddock, his voice booming theatrically across the lawns. "Please take a leisurely stroll around the grounds until all competitors arrive." He indicated with a swoop of his arm the path that led around the perimeter of the gardens, past the rows of vegetables, the greenhouses and henhouse, along the lower gardens with the views of the meadows and hills beyond.

Soon other excited contestants were queuing at the side entrance, some giggling nervously, others standing on tiptoe to look beyond. At the end of the line Alf saw Professor Carmichael. She was surrounded by a group of smiling men and women, all of them, Alf presumed, historians from the Imperial's conference week.

Alf counted the guests. He took out the calculator and worked out takings from entrance fees. He added the likely income from teas, coffees and snacks. Things were going well.

When the draw for the first round had been made, and the first six entrants stood waiting to play, their mallets in their hands, Alf walked into the centre of the lawn.

He couldn't believe this was happening.

He looked up at the line of people on the terrace, at the groups scattered around the lawn.

"Ladies and gentlemen," Alf began, "welcome to the Milton Wells Croquet Tournament. This is a knockout competition and the winner will receive a free weekend at our famous hotel. Let me introduce the very distinguished croquet expert Lord Craddock."

There was spontaneous applause as Craddock

stepped on to the lawn and, as he explained the rules, there was complete silence.

As the first six players stood at the starting line, the spectators grew silent and expectant. The tournament was about to begin.

Alf and Hattie acted as waiters, moving silently between the guests. They ran in with orders, and out with trays of drinks, filling the bar till with coins and notes, and emptying bottle after bottle. Their father returned to the kitchen to finish preparations for the after-match tea.

"Three new bookings!" he shrieked when he saw Alf. "Already! Three people have booked rooms!" Alf grinned and his father did a little jig.

Alf heard the applause, then cheers, then laughter. Lord Craddock announced the next round, and then the third. The warmth of the afternoon was soothed by a gentle breeze, the tension of the competition eased by jokes, laughter and the squeals and groans of competitors.

Finally, with a huge cheer, the competition came to a close. Alf pushed through the spectators with a last tray of drinks and made his way to the front.

In the centre of the lawn Lord Craddock was holding out his arms in triumph. "This perfect afternoon," he exclaimed, "these beautiful gardens, and the management of this excellent hotel have combined to give us a wonderful tournament." The crowd clapped and cheered.

"Now I call upon young Alf Picton, whose idea this was, to come forward to present the trophy."

Alf wasn't expecting this, but he placed his tray upon the grass and strode forward. Craddock winked and, like a magician, produced a small silver cup. He leant forward, passed it to Alf and whispered, "Something I won years ago at snooker, it's cleaned up quite nicely."

Alf turned to face the spectators on the terrace. He took a gulp of air.

"Thank you for making this afternoon such a success," he began. "And I hope you'll all stay for something to eat. Tea will be served on the terrace after the presentation. And don't forget," he was careful to add, "we are a hotel, and have a few rooms still vacant if you are interested in staying."

He noticed some of the spectators turn and nod to each other, some looking up at the hotel.

Lord Craddock stepped forward. He coughed. "The winner of the first Milton Wells Croquet Cup is Professor Helena Carmichael!"

Claps and cheers filled the air, and the professor made her way towards Alf. He smiled and shook her hand, presenting her first with the cup and then a small crumpled envelope from his jacket pocket. "That's your voucher for a free weekend here," he said over the noise of applause, before adding in a whisper, "Have you played croquet before?"

"Thank you, Alf," she said, smiling, holding the cup for a moment before pushing it back into his hands. "Could you display this somewhere in the hotel? Won't you need it for next time?"

"Next time?" said Alf.

"The next tournament," she said. "I hope this isn't going to be the last!"

Alf grinned and Professor Carmichael joined in with the applause.

Craddock put his hand on Alf's shoulder. "I think the day is yours, General Picton," he announced. "What a triumph, what an absolute triumph!"

NINE

The first guest to cross the square was eighty-six-year-old Florence Dickinson. Alf knew she was eighty-six because it was the first thing she told him when she entered reception at a quarter to nine the following morning.

Alf had been up for hours. At seven he made breakfast for his mother and father. He placed two large mugs, a teapot, a jug of milk, boiled eggs and some toast on a tray.

He knocked on his parents' bedroom door. His father appeared, yawning and mumbling to himself, still half-asleep.

"Good grief," he spluttered. "Have you been awake all night?"

At seven-thirty, having emptied the dishwasher, made breakfast and polished Lord Craddock's shoes, Alf set about cleaning the front doors of the Old Forge. Fifteen minutes to do it properly.

Sarah Picton ruffled his hair on her way out. "I'll see you later," she said.

She was off to Wornham College. She turned

and waved to him as she disappeared into North Parade, heading towards the bus stop. His mother seemed a little happier this morning. Perhaps the meditation was helping, after all.

The sun was up over the square. A blackbird sat on Saint Barlow's head and sang cheerfully.

Alf felt as if their luck was changing. Once the brass door handles were gleaming, he began sweeping the entrance. Then he fetched a mop and bucket and began on the steps. Just as he was finishing, Joe Grey, the postman, came loping along the pavement.

"I heard about your big day," said Joe. "Everyone's been talking about it. Long way to go before you match up to the Imperial's standard, though."

"How thoughtful of you to point that out," said Alf, wrapping a hand round the stack of envelopes Joe Grey held out for him.

He looked across the square and Norman Jobson, the Imperial's doorman, stared back at him. Even from where he stood Alf could see Jobson's usual confident expression was strangely absent. Jobson held open the door as guests stepped out, waving away his offer to carry their bags.

Alf watched them for a moment. They were taking a direct route across the square. Two guests from the Imperial were heading straight for the Old Forge.

"I better leave you to it," said Joe Grey. "Looks like you've got customers."

But Alf could only stare. He knew he should run across and greet the women, take their bags from them, escort them into the hotel. But he couldn't quite believe what he was seeing. Coming to his senses, he stuffed the pile of letters into a hole in the hedge, ran in with the mop and bucket and returned to open the front door.

"I'm eighty-six years old," said the first woman as he greeted her. "I'm Florence, and this is my sister, Flora. We came to the croquet yesterday. The garden is so lovely, we've decided to stay here. The Imperial is a very nice hotel, but it isn't very cosy."

Her sister, Flora, stepped up beside her.

"I'm eighty-three," said Flora. "We'd like a room, please."

"Let me take your cases, ladies," Alf said, flashing a genuine smile. "Delighted to welcome you."

He guided them into the reception and asked them to sign in.

"The lounge is just here," he said, "should you feel the need for somewhere to relax. And through there," he said, pointing to the far end of the reception, "is the dining room."

"And where do those double doors lead?" asked Florence.

"The ballroom," said Alf.

"How lovely!" Florence and Flora said together. Alf didn't tell them the room hadn't been used for years.

He led them upstairs to a large room at the back of the hotel. He opened the blinds and windows and cool morning air swept in.

"A view of the garden, and the countryside," said Alf. "Would you like some tea?"

"No, thank you," said Florence, "we had an early breakfast at the Imperial. I think we overdid it. Nothing more now." She held out a tiny hand, two coins pressed between her bony fingers. Alf accepted them and thanked her. Two more for the tip jug.

Alf pulled the door closed behind him.

"Guests," he said to himself. "Two more guests! Two more tips!"

He ran along the corridor and straight into Lord Craddock, who was stepping out into the corridor.

"Careful, Alf!" laughed Craddock.

"Two guests," said Alf, unable to contain himself. "Came across from the Imperial!"

"Splendid! Marvellous! We've got the enemy on the run!"

Dad and Hattie were making breakfast, and jubilation was in the air. Lord Craddock sat on the terrace reading the paper. Purvis was busy in the greenhouse.

Cardew appeared, his beard thicker and blacker.

"I'm going to help Purvis in the garden full time from now on," he announced. "It's our secret weapon, isn't it?"

Alf thought the Welshman needed a shave and a haircut and should stop grinning like a madman. He wondered what the two old ladies would think if they saw him racing around with a hedge trimmer.

"They are very old, aren't they?" said Hattie. "I hope they don't die on us."

When the Dickinson sisters appeared again they looked even smaller and older than Alf remembered. They went straight out on to the terrace and sat at a table. One had a book, the other a pair of binoculars.

Alf served Max and Tilda their porridge and fruit juice in the dining room. He didn't want to say anything to them, but Max spoke first.

"It's very kind of your mother to allow us a meditation room," he said. "She understands the importance of tranquillity; of being able to stop the hands of the clock with just the mind. We all need a haven of peace in this world, don't we, Alf?"

Alf wished he understood what Max was talking about.

Tilda, who rarely said anything at all, held out her hand and rested it on Alf's wrist. "I am sure your mother's kindness will be returned to her," she said. Alf was turning away when the bell in reception rang.

Three people stood by the desk, surrounded by suitcases. For a moment Alf thought Tilda could be right.

A tall man with silver hair and a yellow sweater stepped forward. "Good morning, son," he said. "We were at the tournament yesterday. We had a whole heap of fun." He sounded American. "We were booked to stay at the Imperial until next weekend, but this place has so much more character."

They were Mr and Mrs Richardson from Wyoming. They were touring Europe with their teenage daughter, Ruby.

Within the hour five more guests arrived. All of them had crossed the square from the Imperial. By lunch time that Monday morning, the Old Forge Hotel had thirteen guests. And Alf had been tipped more times in one morning than he could ever remember.

Just after midday Alf was returning downstairs after showing new arrivals to their rooms when he spotted the top hat and bright red jacket of Norman Jobson, who was standing in reception.

"I've heard about your wonderful croquet competition." Jobson rubbed his black-leather-gloved hands together. "You are out of your depth. You have been stealing our customers," he said. "And we don't like that."

He straightened his top hat and adjusted a button on his jacket. He took a step closer to Alf and narrowed his eyes.

"That bellboy costume of yours," he said, waggling a finger at Alf's suit, "has anyone ever told you it's too small for you? That it's full of holes? You look ridiculous."

Alf said nothing; he just wanted Jobson to leave. But Jobson took another step closer.

"You'll be surprised just how nasty things can get," he whispered. He pointed up to one of the wall lights. "This wiring looks terrible. Fire could break out at any time."

At that moment Alf heard a mousetrap snap shut under the stairs.

"Sounds like something has just died in there," said Jobson. "Do your guests know the risks they take staying here? The rats will get them if the place doesn't burn down first."

Jobson smiled and touched his hat, as if saluting a guest. "Good afternoon," he said, and stamped off.

TEN

"No, you don't hold the mallet like a golf club!"
Lord Craddock boomed. He was demonstrating
his croquet technique to the Dickinson sisters.
The sisters giggled, and Alf could see one of them
poke her tongue out behind the old man's back.

It was late afternoon and many of the guests
had gathered on the terrace in the warm sunshine.
Alf and Hattie served drinks.

"Lord Craddock," said eighty-three-year-old
Flora Dickinson, "I don't think this is the game for
us. We're not as young and fit as you."

Alf saw a sparkle in the old man's eye. "Don't
be ridiculous!" he bellowed. "I'm old enough to be
your father!"

Alf stifled a laugh, and was about to make his
way back into the hotel when his father stepped
out on to the terrace.

"Alf," said Tom Picton. "I'd like you to meet Mr
Danks."

"Hello, Alf," said Mr Danks, holding out a podgy
hand for Alf to shake. "I'm the chairman of the

Wornham Croquet Association. It's strange that, although we're only ten miles away, we didn't realize croquet was so alive in Milton Wells."

"Well, we. . ." Alf was about to speak, but then decided it was better to be quiet.

"Anyway," said Mr Danks, "I had a call last night from someone who was here only yesterday and suggested the Old Forge would be an excellent venue for our summer tournament. Do you mind if I take a look?"

Mr Danks snaked through the guests towards the edge of the terrace, Alf and his father following. When Danks reached the balustrade his eyes swept across the scene beneath him, and then into the distance. He nodded in approval.

"My goodness," he said, "the gardens, the views, they are magnificent! And the lawns! They are astonishing. I have never seen such a perfect playing surface." He turned to Mr Picton. "Five days, in mid-August. We'll need about twenty rooms. I don't suppose you could fit us all in, could you?"

Alf could see his father's face freeze over. He was staring at Mr Danks and couldn't speak.

"Let me take you to reception," said Alf, taking control of the situation. "We can make a booking."

Alf felt a shiver of excitement. For a moment

he imagined the hotel full, busier than it had been for years. But just as Mr Danks turned to make his way back into the hotel, there was a shout from the lawn.

"Look! What's that? There, right there!" It was Florence Dickinson.

Alf and Mr Danks looked back. The grass at Lord Craddock's feet seemed to twitch, and then shift slightly, then sink, as if someone was pulling out a plug below the turf.

Crumbs of earth spluttered into the air as they watched. A tiny pyramid of soil appeared.

"It's a mole!" Flora Dickinson squealed.

Sure enough, a tiny molehill began to grow before their eyes. Alf saw Purvis throw down a watering can and come running across from one of the greenhouses.

"Menaces!" Florence howled. "Do something, Lord Craddock!"

"Fear not!" Craddock bellowed. "Always hit the enemy hard!" He grabbed the croquet mallet from the old woman's hand, and, in one graceful but powerful swing, brought it down on the centre of the molehill.

"You wallop it!" Florence urged, flapping her hands and dancing from foot to foot.

"Smack it on the nose!" Flora cried, shaking with excitement.

Craddock released a terrifying shriek and brought the mallet down again, smashing it into the centre of the patch of exposed soil.

Alf heard Hattie scream. "Leave the moles alone!" she yelled, and was about to launch herself over the balustrade towards Craddock.

Tom Picton pulled Hattie back, grabbing her arm. Hattie screamed again and made another lunge.

"You've got it! You've got it!" squealed Florence.

"Lord Craddock!" Flora sighed. "You're marvellous!"

Guests began gathering in a loose circle. Alf could see the astonishment on their faces. Purvis stumbled across the grass, roaring, horrified at the destruction. He knelt by the molehill and rummaged in the soil.

"My lawn," he gasped. "My beautiful lawn."

"Oh, don't be so silly," said Florence. "There are only a few holes."

"And it would have been a far worse mess if Lord Craddock was not such a fine shot!" added Flora.

Eventually Purvis stood up straight, and to the disgust of everyone watching, dangled a velvety black creature from his fingers.

"Monster!" shrieked Flora, staring at the mole.

"Hooligan," said her sister.

Hattie wrenched herself free of her father's grip, climbed over the balustrade and dropped down to the lawn. She walked up to Purvis and held out her hand.

"Is it dead?" she asked.

Purvis held the mole in front of his face. "I think so," he said.

"Of course it's dead," said the old man. "No one messes with Killer Craddock."

ELEVEN

And that was that.

When Sarah Picton returned from college that evening the Old Forge Hotel was almost deserted once more. Alf was the first to tell her what had happened, and when she heard the whole story, she went pale. Alf thought she was going to be sick.

"Tell your father I'm going up to the meditation room," she said. "I can't stand it here much longer."

The Americans left immediately the following morning, and most of the other guests had already gone. Alf scurried across the square with luggage, keeping his head down to avoid Jobson's humiliating gaze. No one pushed a coin into his hand; not one even said thank you.

The Dickinson sisters were the last to go. They asked Alf to call a taxi to take them to the train station. He was relieved they weren't returning to the Imperial.

"We're sorry to go," said Flora, "we know that everyone else was a little frightened by Lord

Craddock's behaviour. But we used to live in the country; we know what moles can do. Lord Craddock was a hero, not a villain."

"We've had a lovely time," said Florence, "and we've had quite enough excitement for ladies of our advanced age."

Later that afternoon, Mr Danks, from the Wornham Croquet Association, rang to explain that he had decided not to go ahead with his booking. He said the behaviour of some of the older guests was not appropriate to the true spirit of croquet.

Everything had gone so well, Alf had felt so close to success. He had almost booked twenty rooms. Now the situation was even worse than it had been before.

Just before the evening meal Alf climbed the stairs to talk to Lord Craddock.

He knocked on Craddock's door and the old man's voice, a little weaker than usual, called him in.

A deep blue early-evening sky filled the windows. The room's lights weren't on, and Alf saw the old man's silhouette sitting on the end of his bed, his head hanging in shame.

"I'm sorry, old chap," he said. "I've been a bit of a fool. I'm going to have to leave. I can't stay now. Your parents must despise me."

Alf looked at the old man, his long, frail body hunched over, his huge hands resting on his knees. "No, sir, they don't. Of course they don't."

"Do you know, Alf," he said without looking up, "I haven't paid them a penny for years. They've let me stay here for nothing all this time. What good, good people they are. And what a fool I am! I will leave first thing in the morning."

"You're not going anywhere," said Alf. He climbed up next to Craddock and put his hand on the old man's back. "You tried, you really did. You wanted to help us. We failed. That's all."

Alf heard Lord Craddock sniff. The old man pulled a large white handkerchief from his pocket; it almost glowed in the pale light. He blew his nose.

Eventually Craddock looked up. "Listen, Alf," he said. "I have to tell you something. Listen, please. I'm a bit of a fraud, you see. I've been a bit of liar and a cheat. Most of my life."

Alf stood up and went to the window. The light was fading and one or two stars were beginning to appear.

"Well, Hattie and I like you, whatever you are," said Alf. "And that's all that matters."

Alf could hear Purvis locking the shed. Cardew was mumbling something about tomorrow. There was the creak of the side gate, and footsteps.

"Well, off you go," said Craddock. "I'm sure your father will be needing your help preparing something to eat. Tell him I'm not very hungry. I'll keep out of the way."

Alf turned to see Craddock standing now, holding out one of his large hands.

"You're a capital fellow," said Craddock. "And one day, Alf, you'll get what you deserve, and what you deserve is a bit of luck." They shook hands. "If anything happens to me, my boy, you must promise never to give up on this place. Never. You mustn't. This place has a special secret, Alf, that is worth more than money can buy." Alf felt his own tiny hand disappear inside the old man's huge fingers.

Craddock looked into the evening sky. "I've been happy here, Alf. Happier than I have ever been before in my life."

"You're a good man, Lord Craddock," said Alf. "Like a grandfather to me." He gave the old man a sudden hug, and then slipped away before anything more could be said.

Downstairs Alf found his father in the kitchen staring into the fridge.

"Where's Hattie?" Alf asked.

"Sitting in her room. She's a bit upset. Needs to be on her own."

"So does Lord Craddock," said Alf. "He doesn't want a meal tonight."

"Fine," said Dad. "The potholers aren't back and Max and Tilda don't want to eat tonight either. I'm going to my workshop."

Alf was left standing alone in the kitchen. The fridge hummed and the light above his head buzzed. Alf wondered if Jobson was right, that the whole place would catch fire and burn down.

And then everything would be gone for ever and he wouldn't have to worry any more.

Alf made himself a sandwich, and took it up to his tiny box room. In bed, he lay awake, the events of the last few days swirling in his head. It would take more than a miracle to rescue the Old Forge. Only some sort of magic could fix things now.

TWELVE

If Alf thought things couldn't get worse, he was wrong. The following day, he woke early to hear raised voices from downstairs.

"Well, I'm not fetching him this time," he heard his mother say. "He'll have to get a taxi."

Alf stood at the top of the stairs. "What's going on?" Hattie asked, coming up behind him. "Has someone died?" she whispered in Alf's ear.

Purvis stood in the centre of reception, looking very miserable.

"I had a bit of an argument with Cardew," he said.

Alf's father came out of the kitchen. "What now?" he said.

"We were in the garden at seven-thirty," said Purvis. "We both wanted to make an early start. First thing he did? He cut through my climbing roses! Thought they were brambles. So I told him he'd never make a gardener. Not in a million years."

"And then what?" said Dad.

"He climbed up on to the roof," said Purvis. "And then fell off again."

Mum groaned.

"I think he's broken his leg," said Purvis.

Dad shook his head. "Where is he now?"

Purvis sighed. "The delivery blokes offered to take him to hospital."

"Delivery blokes?" asked Dad.

"They brought a crate," said Purvis. "It's big. I asked them to leave it just inside the ballroom."

Alf made his way down the stairs, and Hattie followed him. Purvis led the way, and pushed open the ballroom doors. In the centre of the floor was a giant cube: a wooden crate. Dad began wrenching at the top. It opened with a crack. He pulled out giant slabs of foam packaging. The others gathered around to peer in.

"It looks like an egg," said Hattie. "Will it hatch?"

Dad pulled out more packaging and shook his head. "It's a statue of some sort," he said. And after a bit more rummaging he added, "It's a big stone Buddha."

"Well, that's lovely," said Mum. But Alf could tell she wasn't happy. "Max must have ordered it."

"Why?" asked Dad.

"For our meditation room."

"And how much did this cost? Did Max pay for it?"

Mum shrugged. "Look, I need to be going now. I'm already late. I'll see you all later."

"This place is a madhouse," said Dad.

Alf felt uncomfortable. He needed to do something; he missed his routine. He slipped away, gave the front steps a sweep, the main doors a wipe; then he emptied the dishwasher, and began polishing shoes.

Hattie pushed her nose around the door.

"What's going to happen next?" she said. "Do you think we'll be invaded by Martians?"

"Listen," said Alf, "take Lord Craddock his shoes, I need to make some breakfast."

Hattie nodded and did as her brother asked. Alf wanted to be as busy as possible, to keep going. He filled the kettle. He took a loaf of bread from the fridge. He didn't want to stop and have to think what was happening. Things didn't look good, he knew that.

And they were about to get a lot worse.

Hattie screamed.

It was a scream that Alf had never heard before. It seemed to tear through the building, ripping the air.

He dropped the loaf, left the fridge door wide open, and raced upstairs.

Hattie was standing just inside Craddock's room. The shoes had fallen around her. She had her hands over her face and was staring through her fingers towards Craddock's bed.

Alf didn't go in. Hattie was horribly pale, and was crying.

"Alf," she said. "I tried knocking. He usually answers."

Alf felt his teeth bite into his bottom lip.

"He's just lying there, looks like he's asleep," said Hattie. "I tried to wake him up."

Alf still didn't want to step inside the room.

"Alf," whispered Hattie. "I think he's dead."

THIRTEEN

The "For Sale" sign went up the day after the funeral. Alf watched as two men in jeans and T-shirts wired it to one of the pillars at the bottom of the hotel steps.

They grinned and joked as they packed up, pushing their tools into the back of their small white van. It was eight o'clock. These people worked all day putting up and taking down signs.

The sign was hideous: "FOR SALE – Whitby and Callard" in green letters on a yellow background.

Alf hated it and wanted to tear it down. The sign made him feel sick. Then something caught his eye: a red jacket. Norman Jobson stood in the square, a wide grin on his face.

"No one in their right mind will buy that place off you!" laughed Jobson. "My advice would be to give it away. And be quick, before the whole place falls down!"

Alf was too angry to think of what to say. Fortunately, just at that moment, Joe Grey appeared with a stack of mail. Alf watched over Joe's shoulder as Jobson wandered back towards the Imperial.

"I'm sorry about the old man," Joe said to Alf. "There aren't many like him left." He glanced up at the sign and shook his head. "I thought things weren't good here," said Joe. "I have a nose for failure; I can smell it. All these nasty letters you keep getting." He handed Alf a bundle, then held out a thin white envelope with a bright label stuck to it. "And here's a nastier one. Your dad has to sign for this."

"What?" said Alf. He couldn't let his father have any more bad news.

"Someone wants to make sure he reads this," said Joe. "So go and get him to sign this form."

"I'll sign for it," said Alf.

"No, you can't, Alf, it has to be your dad."

"He's busy," said Alf. "Things to do."

"Doesn't matter. Where's your mother?"

"At college. I'll sign it. Let me sign it."

Joe Grey looked one way down the street, and then the other. "I could lose my job over this," he said. He held out a clipboard for Alf. "Just sign it, then. And make sure your dad gets it."

"I will, of course," said Alf.

Alf watched as Joe waddled off down the street. He looked up to check that Jobson had returned to the Imperial, then added the signed-for letter with the wad Joe had already given him and stuffed them all deep into the hedge.

He met his father, who was still in his pyjamas, in the reception. His face was puffy and pale.

"The sign's up," said Alf. "That's it, then, isn't it?"

"They work quickly, those people," said his father.

"You look tired, Dad," said Alf.

"I am. There's a lot to do when someone dies, and I have to sort out poor old Craddock. He had no family we can trace. None at all. I've told Purvis and Cardew we're selling up, that we can't pay them, but they still turn up every day. I think they imagine everything will work out in the end."

"It might, still. Couldn't it?" said Alf.

"Someone's still got to buy the place." His father shook his head and shuffled away.

Later that day Alf found himself in Craddock's room, sitting on the end of the old man's bed. Nothing had been touched.

Alf watched dust swim in the slim blades of light that cut through a gap in the curtains. He remembered someone telling him dust was human skin. Lord Craddock was still there, tiny particles of him, spinning and spiralling in the shafts of sunlight. Craddock had lived in this room for so long it was his home. Everything he owned was in here, all the clues to his past and the man he was.

Perched on the hat stand, like heads bowed in sorrow, were Craddock's glossy top hat, his military cap and two other smaller black hats that probably hadn't been worn for years.

Alf opened the wardrobe and looked at the old man's suits. They were all meticulously pressed and well preserved. He discovered a long black cape and, hidden in the back of the wardrobe, a silver-topped cane. Craddock must have been elegant in his time, whenever that was.

Alf looked through small compartments containing a shelf of belts and braces, another with a razor and shaving brush, one with gloves and scarves. There was an old yellowed cardboard box in there, at the back, and for a moment Alf thought he had found something exciting. But it was just a box of cufflinks.

He sat at Craddock's desk. There was his brush, a comb, a mirror, a writing pad, a cup of pens and pencils. Alf picked up the comb – a long strand of white hair trailed from it. Was this all that was left of the old man?

He pulled open the desk drawers and flicked through a sheaf of dusty newspaper cuttings, a few faded maps and some old magazines. He found several pipes, a watch, a bow tie, a cricket ball, a magnifying glass, a torch and a few pairs of old spectacles. At the back of one drawer was a heap of yellowed crosswords torn from newspapers and magazines, some complete, others half-finished. Craddock's spidery scrawl filled the margins.

There was nothing here that explained much about Lord Craddock. About who he was, or what he did before he came to live in the Old Forge. Alf knew that the old man had been through hard times, but Alf's parents had never been told anything more.

What was it he was looking for? What was he expecting to find? Alf already knew the answer: he wanted to find Lord Craddock. He had a strange sense that if he searched through his things, the old man would appear again. He missed him so much. While Lord Craddock lived, Alf thought the hotel could hang on. Craddock had been living with them for so long he was like a lucky mascot.

"I want you to come back," he said, his voice trembling. "Come back. I want things to be as they were."

He closed his eyes and meant to sit in silence for a while at the old man's desk. But just then he felt a shadow cross the room, and an inky black fog shifting around him. He heard the curtains flap, and the air stirred, moving over his face. A chill swept over him and he sensed there was someone else in the room with him.

"Hattie?" he whispered.

He shouldn't have been going through the old man's things. It made him feel uneasy, a little guilty. He felt as if he was being watched.

Something creaked, a door, a floorboard. Alf's heart thumped in his chest and his pulse drummed in his ears; he was breathing quickly, and his knuckles turned icy cold. He didn't want to open his eyes.

A window hadn't been closed properly; a current of air whistled through a gap, first a hiss, then a whisper.

And then a voice spoke, and Alf knew who it was. It was obvious.

"Alf," it said.

It wasn't Hattie, it wasn't anyone alive.

It was Lord Craddock.

Alf knew he had to open his eyes. If only to make the voice disappear.

"Yes, Alf. It's me."

The voice was clear, and sharp. It sounded as if the old man was there, in the room. But it could have been in Alf's head. He wasn't sure. He wanted Craddock to come back so much, any sound in the room could become his voice.

A shaft of sunlight caught Alf in the face. He tried to open his eyes, but they filled with tears; the light was too bright. He clamped them shut. He shifted position, out of the beam, still recovering from the sudden shock, and held his hands to his face. Kaleidoscopic patterns swirled inside his head.

"Alf," said the voice.

Alf tried to speak but no words would come. His lips were dry; his throat closed. The pulse was still thundering in his head, the blood vessels pumping in his skull.

"I knew I'd scare the living daylights out of you. But I had to come and see you. I need to clear a few things up."

There was a curious smell, like the damp pelt of an animal.

Alf squinted into the room, stood, and reached up at the curtain, pulling it across to cut out the sunlight. Dust coiled about him, and rolled and tumbled. He thought he saw the shape of a dark creature there, spinning through the air. He blinked rapidly, opened his eyes again, and now the loose shape seemed more solid, forming itself into something. This was the shock of the sudden sunlight, surely. There was nothing there. But Craddock's voice came again, out of the murky corners of the room.

"Say something, Alf, please." Alf knew this couldn't be happening, but it seemed real enough. Was he imagining all this? It couldn't be a real ghost, could it? Real ghosts didn't exist. He was expecting Craddock to emerge, or suddenly see the old man, wrapped in his shroud, his face transparent, his lips white, his arms reaching out.

The formless black blob before his eyes curled over itself, spiralling. Alf tried to peer into it, but the blast of sunlight was still disturbing his vision, patches of colour, like islands on a map, spinning and flashing before him.

The draught whistled, Alf shifted his weight and the floorboard creaked. There was something standing over him; he could feel its breath on the back of his neck.

"This place has a special secret, Alf, worth more than money can buy."

Alf was too scared to listen. "Go away!" he shrieked. He slammed his hands over his face.

And just as suddenly the air around him settled. He could breathe fresh air, and the strange stink of fur had disappeared. He knew it had gone.

He jumped up, smacked the light switch on, pulled open the door and threw himself out of the room, dragging the door shut behind him.

Hattie was just coming up the stairs.

"Alf!" she said. "What are you doing in there?"

He could hear her, but he couldn't answer. He had just seen a ghost. A real ghost. He was sure of it.

"Alf," she said again. "Why are you staring like that?"

Perhaps it wasn't real. How could it be?

"Hattie," he said at last. "I've just seen a ghost."

"I knew it!" she said.

"When I was in his room, just now. He spoke to me."

"Lord Craddock?"

"Yes. It was him. I heard him. But it didn't look like him."

Hattie frowned. "So what did he look like?"

"A lump, a dark shape," said Alf. He knew he didn't sound convincing. "A cloud of dust. And it stank."

"Is this a joke?" Hattie said.

"No," said Alf. "I'm serious. I saw a ghost. His ghost."

"I've always wanted to see a ghost," said Hattie.

"Well, I don't ever want to see one again," said Alf.

FOURTEEN

That night the thought of the ghost wouldn't let Alf sleep. He was afraid of closing his eyes. He was afraid of keeping them open. He was afraid the ghost would appear. But at the same time he was afraid it wouldn't.

Alf didn't know what he wanted.

If Craddock returned, he wouldn't be so scared this time. He would ask him difficult questions, ones that only the old man could answer and that Alf didn't know himself, but could check. How many suits did he own? What size shirts did he wear?

And what was it he said, about a special secret?

Or perhaps he had imagined it all. But the voice, and that strange stink. . . They were so real.

Earlier, as Alf had helped his father prepare an evening meal for Max and Tilda, he had wanted to tell his father about the ghost. But something was stopping him. Perhaps it was the feeling that if he talked about it, he would make it more real. Hattie wouldn't say anything, she had promised.

"Max has asked for omelettes," Dad had said. "And as far as I'm concerned he can have whatever he wants tonight. He needs to build up his strength to move that enormous Buddha from the ballroom."

Alf went out to the garden to get some lettuce and then to the greenhouse for tomatoes. The lawn looked perfect in the early-evening light. From inside the coop the hens clucked a welcome to him as he scooped up their eggs and rolled them into his hand.

When he returned to the kitchen his father had some news.

"Professor Carmichael just called. She's claiming her croquet tournament prize: the free weekend. She wants to come and stay."

Alf had mixed feelings about this. He was pleased the hotel would have a new guest, but embarrassed she would be staying when the place was up for sale and so empty.

"Why don't more potholers come?" Alf asked his father.

"They like camping," Dad said, cracking eggs into a bowl. "The ones who stay here are the posh potholers."

"Posh holers," said Alf. "They never seem to be here for long."

Dad laughed. "They like one or two days in the hotel before they get on with the serious business of camping outside. And by the way, where's Hattie? She seems to spend too much time in her room. You don't think it's because of Lord Craddock, do you?"

Alf washed the lettuce, then tore it up before slicing some tomatoes.

"Don't think so," he said. "I think she feels this place is cursed. Whatever we do, it goes wrong. We don't want to leave here, but we can't think of how we can make it work."

"Life's tough, Alf. Running a hotel isn't easy."

They worked in silence for while, then Alf plucked up the courage to ask his father something that had been on his mind. "Dad, what will happen to Craddock's things?"

"I'll have to go through them, then decide what to keep, what to throw away."

"When you do that, will you tell me?"

Dad poured egg mixture into a pan. "Of course. I know how much you liked the old man."

Alf dropped the salad into a bowl, sloshed some dressing over it and took it out to the dining room. He lit a candle on Max and Tilda's table and went upstairs.

He had nothing to do. He emptied the old jug

of coins on to his bed and counted them out. Nine pounds seventy pence. Perhaps this money could go towards a new hobby, something to occupy him. If they had to move to a tiny house, what would he find to do? Experiment with explosives, perhaps. Blow the place up.

He took off his bellboy's uniform and laid it on the chair. Sooner or later, he thought, he'd be taking this suit off for the last time. His grandfather had worn it, and so had his father. He'd be the last one. He knew it was looking shabby these days, but he didn't care. While he still wore it, there was still hope.

He slipped into his pyjamas, turned off the light and got into bed.

What had the voice told him? That the hotel had a special secret worth more than money could buy? Perhaps something was hidden from him, in Craddock's room. Alf imagined pulling up the floorboards, or finding a panel in the wall. Why hadn't the ghost just told him where it was? He wanted there to be a secret, something he could discover. Something to save the hotel, to keep things as they were.

Alf closed his eyes and hoped a message would come in a dream, or that Craddock would return that night and make himself clear.

*

A loud thump woke Alf. He felt his heart race and was immediately wide awake.

"Is that you?" he whispered. He stared into the darkness, trying to find a shape, something he could recognize. He sniffed at the night air, but noticed nothing.

After a while he heard voices. He presumed it was the middle of the night, but didn't know. He got out of bed and stood at his door to listen.

"Watch my fingers!" said a man's voice. It wasn't his father.

"Now!" said another. "Go on, now!"

There was a long, deep scraping sound, as if something was burrowing under the hotel. Alf put his jacket over his pyjamas and pulled out the old watch. It was seven minutes to midnight. He opened his door and listened. There was another bump, then a harsh voice urging someone to be careful.

He moved along the passage towards the first-floor landing. He could hear the voices clearly now; there were three or four of them at least. For a moment he considered the possibility that this was a burglary. His mind began to race. Had they come to find what Craddock had hidden here? Or was it a kidnap? Had they taken Hattie?

He slid along the wall, keeping his eyes on the end of the passage.

And then he saw just a bald, white head appear. It looked like it belonged to an old man, one who was taking a long time getting up the stairs. For a brief moment he was horrified at the thought that this was Craddock. But the head was too round, too white. The face was looking down, as if the old man's back was crooked. Alf expected to see him shuffle forward on a walking stick.

But three other heads appeared, and these were recognizably younger men. They looked hot, as if they were struggling with something.

Then the old white head spun round to face him, and the body appeared, horizontally. Now he recognized him. It was the Buddha.

Three men, one of them Max, were manoeuvring the statue up the stairs, then around the banisters, on to the landing.

"One last push," he heard Max whisper. "We don't want to wake everyone."

"Wouldn't it have been simpler to move it before everyone was in bed?" asked one of the younger men.

"The manager asked if we could shift it at night," Max answered. "He didn't want guests to be bothered." He paused for a moment. "Not that there are any."

Alf watched them edge forward, four contorted faces struggling to shift the stone figure.

"Let me get the door!" squealed Max. "And don't drop it! Watch the skirting board!" Max was just directing now, too red in the face and exhausted to offer any further assistance himself.

Tilda appeared, yawning. She pushed her hand through her hair and frowned.

"It looks very heavy," she said. "Are you sure the floor won't give way beneath it?"

Max shook his head and grinned sardonically at the others. "It's too late for that now," he said. "We're not taking it back down!"

Max and Tilda seemed to do as they liked. Alf hated the way Max grinned and behaved as if he owned the place. He couldn't imagine his father allowing them to bring this huge statue into the hotel, never mind dragging it upstairs in the middle of the night – despite what Max had claimed.

Alf went back to his room and climbed into bed. A few minutes later, as he was drifting off to sleep, he heard a muted cheer and presumed the Buddha was sitting calmly in the meditation room.

He didn't know why Max bothered to drag the colossal thing upstairs when the plan was to sell the hotel. His parents should have told Max to send it back to where it came from. But nothing made sense any more. Lord Craddock had been so straightforward, and now that he was gone, the world seemed populated with adults who behaved in ways Alf didn't understand. He closed his eyes and went to sleep.

FIFTEEN

Professor Carmichael jumped out of the taxi, looking very different to how Alf remembered her. She seemed more relaxed, less businesslike. When she saw Alf, she grinned and waved. He pushed the watch into his pocket. He'd been waiting on the steps of the hotel for twenty-six minutes.

She looked up at the "For Sale" sign. "Oh dear," she said. "Things are not so good, are they? And your father told me about dear old Lord Craddock." But then her expression brightened up. "I've been doing some research," she said as Alf led her through reception. "And I've found out some very interesting things. Just let me get settled in my room and I'll be back down."

Alf grabbed her bags and led her up to a room on the first floor. He had spent the early hours of the morning ensuring it was perfect. He had cleaned and dusted; he had opened the windows, scrubbed the frames. The room was one along from Craddock's. It looked out over the hotel's garden, over fields and distant hills.

Below, Purvis was bending over the coop. Alf assumed he was feeding the hens, and thought he heard him talking to them. Cardew, one arm and one leg in plaster, was leaning on a crutch, watering the vegetables. He looked like a hairy statue.

Alf knew that a couple were coming later that day to view the hotel. His father had scrubbed the front steps, tidied up the reception and cleaned the kitchen. Craddock's room hadn't been touched.

Alf went downstairs and tried to find something to do. He was eager to speak to the professor, but wanted to allow her some time to herself. He sat behind the desk in reception and overheard his father on the phone.

"Yes, the hotel has been in the family for three generations, but my wife has made a successful career as an accountant, and I have an antiques business that is flourishing. The hotel is doing very well, it's just that we've decided to take a new direction."

Alf shook his head. His mother wasn't an accountant yet. His father didn't have a business. The hotel wasn't doing well. His father would say anything to sell the Old Forge; he was desperate.

"Let's go out on the terrace, shall we?" said Professor Carmichael when she reappeared a while later. She was clutching a bulging grey folder.

Alf led her through the dining room and out through the French doors. The professor stood and gazed out over the garden and sighed.

"It is so beautiful here," she said.

"Would you like some tea, professor?" Alf asked.

"Perhaps later," she said. "I want to tell you what I've found out." She patted the folder, then pulled out one of the wrought-iron chairs and sat down at a table. "Come and look," she said, dragging another chair next to hers. "I've discovered something about our friend, the Invisible Claw."

Alf sat down and tried to listen to what the professor was about to tell him, but he couldn't concentrate. He had too much on his mind. He felt the professor studying him closely.

"Is there something you want to tell me about?" she asked.

Alf didn't know where to start. He told her about the decision to sell the hotel, that his father was surprised that someone had shown interest already. He told her about the family's planned move to Wornham and how Hattie had found Lord Craddock, dead. For a moment he thought he might tell her about the ghost.

"You poor thing!" said Professor Carmichael. "I

know you love this hotel. I wish I could help you somehow. You must be so miserable."

"Not miserable," said Alf. "Just confused." And then he decided to tell her. "Professor, do you believe in ghosts?"

She looked slightly alarmed for a moment, then shuffled her papers as if gathering her thoughts.

"No, Alf," she said at last. "I don't. Why do you ask?"

"I've seen the ghost of Lord Craddock," Alf whispered. "Well, not exactly him. A sort of dust cloud, like a creature rolled in a ball. Like a hedgehog. Without spikes. Or a small bear. It smelt like a bear. And it had his voice."

The professor bit her lip and stared at Alf. She reached out and gently put her hand on his.

"Did you like Lord Craddock?" she asked him.

"Yes," said Alf. "I did. He made this place exciting, somehow."

"And you miss him?"

Alf nodded.

The professor smiled warmly, then sat back in her chair and folded her arms. "My father died last year," she said. "And I loved him very much. A few months ago I found myself talking to him. I would be on the way to work, or just going to bed, and I would start chatting away, telling him what I had been doing."

"Did you see his ghost?" Alf asked, and then felt embarrassed.

"No, but I felt he was there. You see, Alf, grief can do strange things to us. And you are dealing with so many other things at the moment."

Alf looked across the garden and tried to remember what it was he had seen in Craddock's room. Perhaps the ghost, or the voice, or whatever he had felt was nothing more than his imagination. But he wasn't convinced.

Cardew was standing in the middle of the vegetables, a hosepipe in his good hand.

"Come on, my beautiful babies!" he pronounced. "Grow huge!"

Alf tried to stifle a giggle. Professor Carmichael, however, hadn't noticed. She had spread photographs, letters and yellowed typewritten pages across the table.

"I've been doing quite a bit of research," she said. "And I'm beginning to realize what went on during the month of the Invisible Claw. Do you remember me telling you the story of the robbery?"

Alf nodded.

She pointed to a black and white photograph of a stern-faced couple dressed in some sort of ceremonial costume. "The king and queen of Pomerania," said the professor. "This photo was probably taken some time before they fled their own country." She picked up the pile of yellowed typewritten pages. "And these are some of the detective's reports. They seem to support the Imperial Hotel's claim that no one there was responsible. The crown jewels were stolen; I knew that. But other guests lost valuable things too, things they had placed in the hotel vault. They blamed the hotel, of course they did." She paused and reached across the table. "And now, look at these."

Professor Carmichael pulled a large envelope from her folder and from it extracted a set of small black and white photographs. She passed them to Alf, one at a time. Each of them showed the same thing: a series of three short lines cut into a floor, a wall and a wood panel.

"This is the only evidence the culprit left behind. These strange gouged lines. They look like the claw marks of an animal, but no animal could do that to stone."

Before Alf could look at all the photographs, the professor lifted a long leather-bound book from the pile.

"But this, Alf, is the best of the lot." She pushed everything else aside and opened the book. "This is the Imperial Hotel's register for that year. As you know, every guest has to sign in, and everyone's length of stay is recorded. Well, you can guess what happened about the middle of the summer, can't you?" She ran her finger down the list of names, turned a few pages. "And here, August the second. Notice something?"

Alf looked closely. He studied the dates of guests' arrivals and departures. And then it hit him. "Everyone's leaving!" he exclaimed. "One by one. And then. . ." He turned the pages quickly. "And for the next few weeks, there are hardly any guests at all!"

"Exactly," said the professor. "The Invisible Claw scared them away!"

Alf felt a thrill of excitement. He knew this was a long time ago, but just imagining guests deserting the Imperial Hotel made him feel warm inside. He threw back his head and laughed.

"But wait a minute," she said. "This isn't all!"

The professor produced a dog-eared newspaper. It was stained and badly creased.

"It became headline news for that summer," she said. "A mysterious, ghostly thief had brought one of the country's most elegant hotels to the brink of ruin."

Alf scanned the stories, looking at the old pictures of sour-faced men and grim police detectives. There was a photograph of the Pomeranian crown jewels and one of the Imperial Hotel as it was all those years ago.

And then Alf realized something.

"Professor," he said, "I think you've just solved an old family mystery!"

He jumped up, ran into the hotel and skidded to a halt alongside the desk in reception. He unhooked the photograph from the wall, then made his way back outside. He laid the large old frame carefully on top of the professor's papers.

"These are my great-grandparents, Albert and Mary, on the steps of the hotel many years ago. And there's my grandfather, George, when he was a boy."

"He looks so proud," said the professor. "He can't be more than six or seven."

Alf patted his jacket. "This suit was made for George, when he was much older. And this belonged to him, too." He pulled out the silver fob watch. He tapped the photograph. "Look, my great-grandparents are holding the trophy for 'Milton Wells' Hotel of the Year'. My dad told me that George was too young to remember what happened back then, and Albert died long before Dad was born. But that was the only year the hotel has ever won the trophy."

"Let me guess," said the professor, "the Imperial has won it every other year?"

"Of course." Alf scowled. "But I've always

wondered how Albert and Mary did it. And now I think I know how."

The professor studied the photograph.

Alf wanted to shout but he was so excited his voice was trembling. "We won the trophy that year because so many guests had left the Imperial and stayed here."

The professor looked up at him.

"And now we know who helped us win the cup!" he said.

The professor grinned and nodded.

Alf was almost jumping around the table now. "It was the Claw! The Invisible Claw! The Old Forge Hotel must have been full that summer! Full to bursting!"

"Alf!" the professor cried. "This is wonderful! I was thinking of writing my book about the strange events at the Imperial, but now it seems as if the Old Forge is the key to the mystery! Can you find the hotel's registers for that year?"

"All that stuff is in the attic," said Alf. "Perhaps we'll find the Invisible Claw was staying here too!"

SIXTEEN

The bulb in the attic flickered. Alf pushed an old suitcase across the floor, causing a blanket of dust to billow out. A column of magazines teetered precariously, only propped up by an ancient wireless. He stepped over a grimy electric radiator, then nudged a pram with his foot, keeping his face out of the disturbed air. An old card table lay on its side. Alf levered it out of his way and squeezed through. Here he found a row of cardboard boxes. Large, dark dog-eared volumes lay inside: the hotel registers. He prised one of the books out and, holding his breath, leafed through it.

One by one he went through them until he found what he was looking for. It wasn't a simple task. Each register covered more than one year; some spanned five or six. There was nothing to clearly indicate which was which, the light in the attic was poor, and the writing inside so small and spidery.

But it was there. It was identical to all the

others, just as impregnated with dust, just as frayed at the spine.

He switched off the light and moved back down the steps, the heavy register gripped tight and pinned under his arm.

When he reached the first floor he stopped, realizing he was caked in attic grime. He set down the book and took off his jacket. It was filthy. He began flicking at the dust and picking off thick strands of ancient cobwebs.

Hattie appeared from nowhere.

"I hate you," she said.

"What?"

"You've been setting traps, haven't you? I heard one go off, and I found this." She held out her palm. A dead mouse lay there. She pushed it under his nose.

"Like dead things, do you?"

"I thought you did," he snapped. "You seem to like burying them."

"I hate things dying!" Hattie cried. "I hate death. I bury these poor creatures because it makes me feel better. But you did set the traps, didn't you?"

Alf nodded. "Sorry," he said.

"And what are you doing in the attic? The professor's here, isn't she? How do you suppose she's going to help us?" She stared hard at him, narrowing her eyes. "There are people coming to look at the hotel this afternoon. Did you know that? They might buy it! We have to stop them. We don't need a professor, we need Lord Craddock's ghost, or evil spirits, or something to frighten everyone away. . ."

She stopped suddenly as a low rumbling came from below them. Alf felt the floorboards shake, even buckle slightly. Hattie looked up. Above them they heard something crash down, like an ironing board, and the building shuddered.

"Is Cardew on the roof again?" said Hattie.

"Not with a broken leg, surely," said Alf.

There was a crunch and a loud screech as if huge timbers were about to split apart. Alf sensed the hotel was leaning, or twisting.

"What's happening?" said Hattie, her eyes wide and frightened.

Alf waited for a moment; everything seemed normal. But then the floor and ceiling began to shake and the judder came again.

They stood staring at each other, waiting for the sound to return. This time it was louder and more disturbing. It seemed as if something was shifting, unsettling the whole building. Windows rattled, tiny flakes of plaster fell from the ceiling.

"Is it an earthquake?" said Hattie, her face pale and anxious.

"Don't know," said Alf. "But it feels like

something is about to go." He was half expecting to see the ghost of Craddock appear at any moment, hovering there, his pipe in his mouth, his tiny eyes glistening.

The thought flashed through his mind that he had disturbed something in the attic. Perhaps he had knocked a joist, or something that was responsible for holding up the roof.

He picked up the book. "Come on, Hattie," he said. "I think we'll be safer outside."

Brother and sister slipped back downstairs into reception, where everything seemed quite normal. Their father was standing by the front door.

"Didn't you hear that noise?" said Alf. "Everything upstairs was shaking."

"We've had a dry few weeks," said Dad. "The woodwork starts to shrink, makes strange sounds. My father used to say he sometimes felt he was in an old ship at sea."

Alf nodded. It did sound like that.

Hattie and Alf scuttled through the dining room to the garden. Professor Carmichael was still sitting on the terrace, reading, and when she heard the children she turned to greet them. She was wearing glasses now, and she peered over the top of them.

"Hello again," she said to Hattie. "Do you remember me?"

Hattie nodded.

"I think this is what you were looking for," said Alf, holding out the register.

"Right." The professor grinned. "Come on, sit down, both of you."

As Professor Carmichael began leafing through the register, Alf told Hattie about their discovery.

"We think we know why the Old Forge won the cup all those years ago," he said. "And it may have something to do with the unsolved mystery of the Invisible Claw. That was the last time the Old Forge was the best hotel in Milton Wells. Perhaps we can find some way of doing it again!"

Hattie, still clutching the dead mouse, was about to speak when a thunderous roar came from somewhere inside the hotel, as if the building was being torn open. The sound rolled around inside, windows shook, slates fell, glass shattered.

"What on earth was that?" said the professor.

Alf jumped up. He heard Hattie call from behind him but ran in, oblivious to the danger. Flakes of ceiling were falling around him; he could taste plaster and dust. He found his way through to reception. It was deserted.

"Dad?" he called out.

"Alf!" his father replied. "What's going on?"

A puff of white dust emerged from under the

door of the lounge. Whatever had made the terrifying sound was in there.

Alf looked back at his father, who stepped forward and gripped the handle of the door. He pushed it open.

"What. . .?" was all Alf heard his father say. An impossibly huge grey cloud billowed out and into the reception, leaving everything layered in fine chalky dust.

Alf stepped into the room, and realized Hattie was behind him.

Whatever it was, it had come from the far end of the lounge, just in front of the bay windows, where the dust was thick and swirled like a muddy pond. A dreadful silence, like the aftermath of a bomb blast, hung in the room. Now and then pieces of rubble fell and rattled through loose floorboards.

"Hello? Hello?" Professor Carmichael's voice called out. She joined them, standing there in the sea of dust, the shreds and wisps of debris, the dark hole of the blasted lounge. Then came Purvis, and the faltering steps of Cardew, whose beard gathered the fine powdered plaster so quickly he seemed to age in seconds.

"Has something exploded?" the Welshman growled.

And as they watched, and as the dust settled

around the devastation, each one of them began to realize what had happened.

There he was, looking like he had just burst up out of the floorboards. He was tilted at a slight angle, so that one shoulder was higher than the other, and his eyes were closed as if he couldn't bear to see what he had done. The Buddha sat in a gaping hole, and had dragged down most of the carpet with him.

Alf realized that the strange sounds he and Hattie had heard earlier must have been the floorboards giving way. The statue of Buddha had plummeted through the ceiling from the meditation room above, then crashed down, tearing through the carpet, ripping out nails and splintering woodwork.

The Buddha's bald, domed head, layered in dust, poked out from a deep, jagged crater.

"Your mother isn't going to believe this," said Tom Picton.

"Could have killed someone," said Purvis.

"I could have broken my other leg," said Cardew.

"What are we going to do?" Hattie cried.

But Alf was smiling. "There's no way we can sell the hotel now."

SEVENTEEN

The rain came that afternoon. As the job of clearing the plaster and rubble from the devastation in the lounge began, thunder rolled over Milton Wells and lightning cracked against the bleak sky.

Sarah Picton arrived home that evening, soaked and miserable. After she'd seen the Buddha and the hole in the ceiling, it was an hour before she could speak.

And just as they were sitting down to eat, the electricity shut off.

Tom sighed. He disappeared for a few moments to make a telephone call. When he returned he looked concerned. "We've been cut off," he announced. "The bill hasn't been paid. They say they've sent us three demands. Well, I haven't seen them. Come to think of it, we haven't received many bills lately. I don't understand."

Alf looked away.

Dad produced some candles, set them into holders and lit them. He handed out bowls and ladled soup into them. A plate of warm rolls sat in the centre of the table. Alf offered them around.

"When I write my book," said the professor, "I will have to include this little story. People won't believe it."

"The adventures of the fearless flying Buddha," said Cardew. He took a roll and pulled it apart, then shoved one half into his mouth.

"How will we get it out of the hole?" Alf asked.

"Get some lifting gear," said Dad. "It'll pop out like a cork from a champagne bottle."

But the Buddha had given Alf hope. Until the lounge was properly cleared up, the ceiling and floor repaired and the room redecorated, the hotel could not be sold. He still had time to save the Old Forge. A few more weeks, Alf thought, and anything could happen.

He was thinking this as he climbed into bed, his hair full of plaster, his skin layered in dust, thunder still booming over the hills, the rain hammering against the window.

The room began to feel colder, and he recognized a damp, earthy smell. It could have been the rain, but Alf felt uncomfortable. He pushed himself down under the quilt and peered over the top.

The window rattled, and something outside toppled over, a dustbin perhaps.

Alf stared into the darkness above his head, into a black whirlpool that was forming against the ceiling. The shape rolled above him, and began transforming itself. He saw a weird, acrobatic creature, spinning, somersaulting, and the stink of damp fur was everywhere. It was the ghost.

"Alf," said Craddock's voice.

And then he realized what he was looking at. A mole. A floating ghost mole.

"Yes, I know, it's barmy, isn't it?" said Craddock. "We've become a bit mixed up, the mole and me."

Alf stared hard. This couldn't be real.

"Suppose it was all my fault," said Craddock. "Shouldn't have belted the poor fellow."

The mole ghost hung above Alf's head, like a parachutist in free fall, its huge claws extended like paddles, its glossy snout wrinkling when it spoke.

"I'm a real ghost," said Craddock. "A real ghost mole. You'd better get used to it."

"This can't be happening," Alf whispered. "It's crazy. Everything's gone mad!"

"Now, come on, old chap," said the mole, "you should be jolly delighted. That business with the Buddha fellow, the ceiling collapsing, well, it's given you a stay of execution."

"Yes, I know," said Alf. "Why don't you tell me something I don't know? Prove you're real. You said something about a big secret. What is it?" He sat up in bed and watched in disbelief as the mole drifted down through the darkness and dropped on to the quilt. It opened its tiny eyes, blinked, then raised a claw and scratched its head.

"I can't!"

"Why not?" said Alf. "Why can't you tell me anything?"

"It wouldn't be right. That's not what ghosts do!"

"Well," said Alf, deliberately yawning and stretching his arms. "In that case I'm going back to sleep."

"No, you can't!"

"I am! I might as well if you won't help."

Alf tried to lean forward to study the creature. The more he looked, the less obvious it was to him he was looking at a mole. It could have been a fold in the quilt, or a shadow of a pattern in the curtains. But then it spoke again.

"Alf!" said the mole. "Listen to me. I can tell you this. Don't give up! You're so close! You will save the hotel, and so much more. Haven't you found out about me yet? Are you looking carefully enough? Remember what I always told you. The answers are staring you in the face!"

"What do you mean?" Alf asked, frustration rising in his voice. "Look, if you know something, just tell me."

"I'll give you a clue. Look on the cup," said Lord Craddock. "Got that? *Look on the cup*, Alf."

Alf tried to reach out and grab the thing, but as his fingers closed around the black shape, the mole shot up, somersaulted, and was gone.

EIGHTEEN

Banging woke Alf the following morning.

He pushed open the lounge door to find builders setting up scaffolding below the hole in the ceiling. One was hammering a bolt into place. The Buddha's head still poked out of the floor, leaning at an angle.

Alf discovered Professor Carmichael making herself some coffee in the kitchen. She was looking less like a professor every day. Her clothes were a little crumpled, and her hair, though tied back, was unwilling to behave: unruly strands headed off on journeys of their own.

"I don't suppose I should be in here," she said. "But there is no one else around. You don't think your mum or dad will mind, do you?"

Alf shook his head. "It doesn't make much difference now," he said.

"I need to stay a few more days; I hope that'll be all right. I'll pay, of course. I've made a little breakthrough, Alf," she said. "A newspaper cutting. Wait until you see it."

"What about the old register? Have you discovered anything more?"

"Yes, just how well the Old Forge did in the summer of the Claw."

"I'm not surprised," said Alf. "They must have thought the Imperial was. . ." And then he realized what he was about to say and stopped.

Professor Carmichael looked at him suspiciously. "What were you going to say?" She took a sip of her coffee.

"Nothing," said Alf. "Doesn't matter."

"Were you going to say 'haunted'?" He knew she couldn't be fooled.

"Yes," said Alf.

"Have you seen the ghost again?" she asked him.

Alf nodded. "Last night. And it's a ghost mole, now."

"What?" The professor stifled a smirk.

"The first time I didn't realize what it was. This time it was obvious. It was a mole. A mole with Lord Craddock's voice."

The professor couldn't disguise her astonishment. "Have you told your parents?"

Alf shook his head. "It would only give them another reason to leave."

"You know I don't believe in ghosts," said the professor, "so I think there must be some sensible explanation. Did it say anything?"

"I know I must be imagining it," said Alf, "but there was one thing."

"Yes?"

"He said, 'Look on the cup.'"

"Cup? What cup?"

"Well," said Alf, "I suppose he means the Hotel of the Year trophy. It's in the photograph on the wall in the reception, but it's not possible to read anything on it. It's far too small."

The professor laughed. "This is very odd. Perhaps I should go and look at the real trophy. I expect it's on display in the Imperial Hotel somewhere, if they still have it."

"They do," said Alf. "The mayor presented it to them at the end of last summer. They make sure the photographs get in the paper, every year."

"Well, I'll see if I can go and take a look at this magnificent trophy," she said.

"So you believe me?" Alf asked.

"You could know something without realizing it," said the professor. "Our memories are very powerful. Perhaps, when you were younger, you heard something, or saw something, that suggests there is a clue on the cup. That's what could have put the idea in your head. But, Alf, there are no such things as ghosts. You haven't seen a ghost and it wasn't a ghost that drove people away from the Imperial Hotel all those years ago. It was a thief. A very clever thief. Someone who could slip in and out without being noticed."

"Or someone who was there all the time," said Alf. "One of the guests."

"They were all interviewed, I know that. Their rooms were searched, nothing was found. When the Pomeranian crown jewels went missing, the hotel was locked from the inside, and detectives were called. The place was turned upside down. The manager must have known it would reflect very badly on the hotel if nothing turned up."

"But the jewels were never found?"

"No," said the professor. "The Invisible Claw made himself, and everything he took, disappear into thin air."

"And if the Claw was one of the guests, did he change hotels too, and come and stay here?"

"He could have. The Imperial emptied, and every single one of the guests registered at the Old Forge. I've checked. That surprised me, because the Imperial is so much bigger. But it wasn't then. It's more or less doubled in size since the summer of the Claw. Now, come on," said the professor, rinsing out her coffee mug.

"I've some very interesting things to show you."

Heavy rain battered the windows of the professor's room, and the dark, overcast sky made it seem like a winter evening. A desk lamp provided the only light. At least the electricity was back on.

The professor had spread her books, papers and photographs on every available surface.

"There's the list of guests from the Imperial," she said, handing Alf two sheets of paper. "You'll see I've added how long they stayed in each hotel, and the dates they left. But wait until you've seen this." She took the lists of guests from him and with a dramatic flourish produced a narrow strip of newspaper.

"Someone at the university did some work for me. It's incredible what can turn up."

The rain was pouring off the roof. Alf could hear great torrents spilling from the gutters. He held the cutting in the light from the desk lamp and began to read. The paper was yellowed and brittle. The headline said:

IS THIS THE INVISIBLE CLAW?

Below it was a black and white photo of a man with a long, handsome face and a large black moustache.

Police believe they have arrested the criminal responsible for a series of unsolved robberies committed across the country and stretching back for over three years. Percival Merriweather, aged twenty-seven, presently residing in London, was caught by police breaking into a jeweller's in Kingston, Surrey. Merriweather had used an adjoining sewer to tunnel through to the property.

After a recent spate of burglaries in the area, the jeweller had decided to spend the night at the premises. When woken in the middle of the night, he was shocked to discover the floor of his shop being broken up from below. The police were summoned and were present as Merriweather emerged into the room.

On closer inspection of his tools, the police discovered a large and unusual hammer, which, when used to cut into stone, produces three scored lines, as left by the infamous crook known as the "Invisible Claw".

"So that's him?" said Alf.

"Maybe. I don't know what happened in court, what the sentence was or where he went to prison. I'll have to work on that."

"And this name, Merriweather," said Alf. "It doesn't appear anywhere in the registers?"

"No," said the professor. "Perhaps he stayed here under an assumed name. Or was never a guest at all. Perhaps he tunnelled into the Imperial from below. The marks left behind are very unusual and match those of the hammer used in the Kingston robbery. If it wasn't the same man, it was certainly the same hammer." She passed him a large black and white photo. "Look, this is it. Merriweather even gave it a name."

Alf took the photo and sat down on the end of her bed. It showed the hammer, about thirty centimetres long, big enough to be its actual size. Etched into the wooden handle in dark capital letters were the words "THREE OF GOLD".

"Strange thing to do," said Alf. "Name a hammer."

"The three-clawed hammer," said the professor, "that led him to the gold."

"Why would he name it? Wouldn't it be like admitting he was the thief?" Alf passed the photo back to her. He couldn't help but show his disappointment.

"What's the matter?" asked the professor.

"How can this help us?" he said. "I hoped you'd made a discovery that would help you write a book. Make us famous. Save the hotel."

The professor sat down next to him. "I'm sorry, Alf," she said. "I can't pretend any of my investigations will make much difference. Perhaps I shouldn't stay."

"No, please don't go. Everything seems so mad at the moment. You're the one thing that seems normal."

"Well, compared to a talking ghost mole, I suppose I am."

"And you really think what I'm seeing is just my imagination? An imagination that tells me to look for clues on the Hotel of the Year trophy?"

"Exactly," said the professor. "I am a historian; I have to rely on evidence, not the supernatural. And now I'm going to smarten myself up and go and ask if I can take a look around the Imperial, see if I can find that cup. There's a mathematicians' conference going on at the moment. It's never quiet over there, is it?"

"No," said Alf. "Not like it is here."

NINETEEN

The professor returned from her visit to the Imperial with disappointing news. She had found the cup; the hotel manager was only too delighted to show it to her. It sat on a shelf behind his desk. She had looked at the cup closely, but it was unmarked. There was no inscription, no dates, nothing. The ghost mole had sent them on a wild goose chase.

Alf kept staring at the photograph of Albert and Mary and the staff on the steps of the hotel. He couldn't take his eyes off it. He had hoped that the cup would yield its secrets. Outside the rain hammered down on the pavement. In the photograph the sun was still shining.

Then the front door swung open and a rush of wind and rain gusted into the hotel. Three figures came in, waterproof jackets zipped up against the wet, hoods dripping. Their faces were deep in their collars; they looked soaked and uncomfortable.

"Hello, Alf," said one. "Camping is grim in this weather. Any spare rooms?"

Alf recognized the potholers. "Yes," he said. "Sure. You can have the same rooms as you had before."

"Oh, it's not just for us," said the second. "Mill Hole field has started to flood. There are a few more of us outside."

"Well, tell them to come in," said Alf.

The tallest of the three went to the door, pushed it open, and yelled into the rain. To Alf's astonishment, a line of soaking campers, some in potholing gear, some with their equipment on their backs, others with tents rolled under their arms, gathered in the reception.

"Dad!" shouted Alf, staring at the sodden horde. "I think you should come in here a minute."

Tom Picton appeared, a piece of sandpaper in one hand, his face crumpled from concentrating on a repair.

"What is this?" he said at last.

"Guests," said Alf.

The tall potholer stepped up to the desk. "I've told them what a perfect place this is for us. Not too precious. And Alf here, he's a star. Can you fit us in?"

"How many, exactly?" asked Alf's dad.

The potholer pulled down his hood and scratched his chin. "About forty of us," he said.

TWENTY

The Old Forge Hotel was almost full and Alf was busy again. As he showed each new guest to their room, he ran through the breakfast menu and informed them that room service was available; he would be delighted to bring them teas, coffees or a light snack at any time. Would they like a newspaper? Was there any mail they needed posting? If shoes or boots were left outside the bedroom door in the evening they would be clean by morning. Nothing would be too much trouble. He would be delighted to be of service.

And he was delighted. He ran up and down the stairs, grinning and chuckling, his feet barely touching the ground. His pockets jangled with tips.

Cardew announced that, despite his injuries, he would resume cooking. Purvis brought in cardboard boxes brimming over with tomatoes, lettuces, cabbages and onions. A pyramid of eggs sat in a huge bowl above the fridge.

Alf and Hattie were sent out shopping. "They are going to be hungry," Tom Picton reminded them, "and if the campsites are flooded there may be even more arrivals."

At Blake's, the tiny supermarket on North Parade where their mother worked on Saturdays, yellow light spilled out on to the wet pavement. They swept along the aisles, filling their trolley with anything they thought the hungry potholers would appreciate. Teetering towers of pies, mountains of bread, puddings and cakes, columns of biscuits, wedges of cheese and cubes of butter sat in the trolley at the checkout.

They hauled the shopping back to hotel, where their mother, her hair plastered to her head with rain, stood in reception staring at the maze of wet footprints. "What's that horrible damp smell?" she asked the children as they pushed in through the main door.

"Guests," said Alf, beaming.

At breakfast the following morning Cardew and Tom Picton were cracking eggs, grilling bacon, brewing tea and coffee. Alf and Hattie danced between them, transporting plates piled high into the dining room.

Alf placed his watch on the tray he carried, now and again glancing at the second hand.

Five breakfasts could be rolled out every six

minutes; a fresh pot of tea in just under three. When the grill was red-hot it took just under two minutes to toast eight slices of bread.

The new arrivals cheered when their meals arrived, rubbing their hands together in expectation. They fought for the tomato sauce, wolfed down sausages and gulped steaming coffee. They spooned jam and honey on to their toast; they bellowed their thanks with exuberant voices. The dining room hadn't been as noisy for years, and Alf loved it.

Professor Carmichael told Alf she needed to conduct some investigations. "I want to find out what happened to our friend Merriweather," she whispered secretly when he presented her breakfast on a tray at the door of her room. Alf noticed it was even more of a mess. "So I'll be gone for most of the day. But we'll catch up later, OK?"

Alf's mum announced she would be suspending her studies for a while. Forty new guests were an opportunity to make some money. As breakfast was coming to an end, she began making preparations for lunch, counting the places, checking the freezer, then sitting at the desk in the office and going over figures.

Cardew and Tom Picton began clearing things away, arguing over the music that they played in the kitchen. Despite the rain, Purvis worked outside, plucking beans and pulling up potatoes, weeding, clipping hedges, scraping moss from walls and throwing slugs and snails into old buckets.

After lunch some of the potholers sat in the dining room playing cards or chess; others disappeared to their rooms. Alf maintained his presence, offering them tea, biscuits and cakes, or asking them if they needed anything from the shops in North Parade.

Many of them worked at crosswords and enjoyed the competition of finding the answers first.

"OK, Alf, help us with this," whispered one of them. "Listen to this clue: *a ruined orange vest can still be used as a memorial.*"

Alf pulled a face. "I don't get it," he said.

The potholer explained. "If a crossword clue uses a word like 'ruined' or 'broken up' or 'smashed', it means the words that come next are probably an anagram."

"What's that?" Alf asked.

"Well, here we have to solve how to rearrange the letters of the words *orange vest* to make another word."

Hattie came in with a tray of orders. She looked over Alf's shoulder.

"A ruined orange vest can still be used as a memorial," repeated one of the potholers.

"Doesn't make any sense to me," said Alf.

"Gravestone," Hattie announced.

"What?" said Alf.

"That's it!" The potholer grinned. "Hattie, you've got a gift."

Alf looked at his sister. "How did you work that out?"

"I just saw the letters of *orange vest* could be moved about to make *gravestone*. Smart, aren't I?"

Another potholer, overhearing Hattie's solution, called her over. "What about this clue? *Smash up modern truths and run for cover*."

Hattie blinked a few times and then said, "Thunderstorm!"

The potholers burst into applause. Alf looked confused. "I don't get any of this!" he shouted over the clapping.

"The clue means smash up the words *modern truths* to make something else. The letters of those words can be made into *thunderstorm*. And if there's a thunderstorm, you run for cover!"

Alf looked from one potholer to the next; they were all nodding in agreement.

Tom Picton opened up the bar and began serving drinks, and for most of the afternoon the hotel had the atmosphere of a big family party. No one was enjoying it more than Alf.

Max and Tilda crept downstairs to ask if food could be sent to their room. The builders ate their packed lunches in the debris and dust of the lounge, but Alf didn't neglect them, taking in a tray of tea and a plate of biscuits.

Later, in the lull between the excitement of the afternoon and the evening meal, Alf slipped outside to stand on the steps of the hotel. The rain fell noisily on the broad leaves of the plane trees around the square. People hurried along the wet pavements, hidden under umbrellas, or had their faces set deep into upturned collars of raincoats. Outside the Imperial Hotel, sheltering under the awning, Norman Jobson stood hunched up in his black top hat and vivid red coat. The lights of the Imperial shone around him, and over the wet stone steps.

This was a proud moment for Alf, and he wanted to savour it. He knew the potholers were staying for only as long as it rained. But for now, just for a day or two, the Old Forge Hotel was as busy as its rival across the square.

A young couple in anoraks with rucksacks dripping on their backs splashed along the pavement. They turned their faces up to the Old Forge. They looked wet through and miserable.

"Good evening," said Alf. "Why don't you come in and dry off? I'll make you a hot drink, and some sandwiches."

The couple smiled and looked relieved. Alf opened the door for them and followed them in. He helped them with their rucksacks, and suggested they put their things around the radiator. He led them to the dining room. The crossword-mad potholers were still trying to complete their puzzles, the chess-playing potholers still studying their pieces, but most had gone up to their beds.

When Alf took the couple their tea, the young woman asked if there were any rooms available for the night.

"I'll just check," said Alf.

His mother was tidying the office.

"One more couple, Mum," said Alf. "Can we fit them in?"

She smiled, shook her head in disbelief, and ushered Alf into the small space behind the reception desk. She ran her hand down the register, then handed him a key.

"And now, Alf," she said, her eyes glistening slightly, "you can tell anyone else that the Old Forge Hotel is full."

At that moment Tom Picton came out of the kitchen. He was wearing an apron, and looked flushed and excited.

"Dad," said Alf. "We're full up! No vacancies!"

"Excellent," said his father.

"Perfect," said his mother.

Something in this exchange concerned Alf. "What's going on?" he asked.

"We have a possible buyer coming later this week," said Mr Picton. "We know the lounge is still a mess, but. . ." He paused and looked at his wife.

"Alf," she said. "You've worked hard, and the reason we're doing so well is down to you. Your father and I are so pleased. It couldn't have come at a better time. It'll be so much easier to sell the hotel now that it's full."

TWENTY-ONE

"We can't win!" Alf told Hattie. She was sitting on her bed, a sketchbook balanced on her knees. Alf sat on a stool, staring out of the window. Hattie kept trying to draw him.

"Keep still," she snapped.

"If the place is empty, Mum and Dad say we're not making any money, so it's pointless staying here," said Alf. "And if it's full, then they say it's a good time to sell."

"Stop talking," said Hattie. "I'm trying to do your chin."

"We're full," said Alf. "Can you believe it? Every room – well, not the junk room on the second floor, or Craddock's, and not the room with the hole in the floor, but we're. . ."

"Alf, shut up and let me draw you!" demanded Hattie.

Alf tried to keep still. His head swirled with the events of the last few weeks: the croquet competition, Craddock's death, the ghost mole, the Buddha's plunge, the potholers and the Invisible Claw.

"Your nose looks bigger," said Hattie suddenly. "And you're getting a crease on your forehead."

"Thanks," said Alf.

"It's funny," said Hattie, "as people get older some bits of their face change, but not others. I think eyes hardly change at all. When you look at photos of Mum and Dad when they were young, they have the same eyes."

"What do you think we'll be doing when we're their age?" Alf asked her.

"Please don't speak," Hattie protested, "I'm drawing your lips now." She thought for a minute. "Well, I've just decided I'll be an artist. And I'll draw animals and things like that for science. I'll work in South America and on the Pacific Islands. And you'll be waiter in a café in Wornham. I'll come and see you now and again."

The late-afternoon skies hung heavy and dark over Milton Wells, promising more rain. Alf hoped it would rain for ever, that the guests would never go, and that his parents would change their minds. But deep down he knew whatever happened, they would be selling up and leaving very soon.

"Right," said Hattie, "I'm drawing your eyes now. You can talk, but don't blink."

"I hope that person doesn't turn up," said Alf.

"The person who wants to buy the hotel?" said Hattie. "They must be mad. The place is falling down."

"Falling down," said Alf. "But full."

"Only until it stops raining; then the potholers will all go back to their tents."

"But someone looking to buy the hotel wouldn't know that," said Alf.

"Well, I'll tell them," laughed Hattie. "And you're blinking."

"If you tell them," said Alf, "Mum and Dad might have to accept less for the hotel. And then we'll end up living in a tiny flat in Wornham. We'll have to share a bedroom. No garden. No graveyard."

"I won't tell them, then," she said. "I'll keep out of the way."

"That's what I mean," said Alf. "We can't win."

"Finished," said Hattie, slapping her pencil down.

"We are," said Alf.

"I meant my drawing, silly," said Hattie. She picked up the drawing pad and turned it to show Alf.

"I look about fifty!" Alf snapped.

"No, you don't!" laughed Hattie.

Alf stood at the window. "So what do we do?"

"Give up," she said. "I have. Think of something

else you'd like to do. That suit of yours is almost in pieces anyway."

Alf looked down at the jacket. One or two buttons were beginning to come loose. In the light from the window he could see the blue material was covered in ugly stains. The sleeves were far too short for him and the cuffs were badly frayed.

"I'm not going to give up, Hattie. And you shouldn't either. I love every brick of this hotel. It's my home, it's all I've known. It's all I want to know."

"Great speech," said Hattie, pushing herself up from the bed. "But it doesn't get us anywhere."

"This place is special," said Alf. "I know it is, you know it is. We just have to find that thing that makes everyone else know it; something that makes it impossible for Mum and Dad to sell up."

"Like a Buddha buried in the lounge floor?" said Hattie. "That's quite unusual." She stood next to him and put an arm on his shoulder. "Or a chef who climbs on the roof when someone's nasty to him?"

"Something that will make everyone hear of us, make us world famous."

"You'll have to get a new uniform if that happens," said Hattie.

TWENTY-TWO

Professor Carmichael didn't appear for breakfast the following morning. After waiting another half an hour Alf took a tray of coffee to her room. He knew she had been late coming in the night before, and might not want to be disturbed. But he felt time was running out. His parents were expecting someone they thought might be interested in buying the hotel. If anyone was going to rekindle his hope that a miracle might save the Old Forge, Alf felt it would the professor.

He knocked and called her name. When she eventually pulled open the door she was wrapped in a huge white bathrobe, and her eyes looked puffy. "Sorry, Alf, I didn't mean to sleep so late. Come in, please."

The curtains were still drawn and the room was in darkness. The professor switched on the light and crouched down beside a pile of folders and papers.

"Last night, I came across something. I think I

know what happened to Percival Merriweather. Now, where did I put it?"

Alf couldn't help but smile at the heaped mound of papers. He stood next to her table, the tray in his hands, watching her rummage through them. He remembered first seeing her, the day she came to the Old Forge, mistaking it for the Imperial. She looked so severe then, so organized. Now she looked a little batty. Alf liked that.

"Here it is!" she cried, pulling out a sheet of paper from a folder. She placed it on the table, took the tray from him and sat down to drink her coffee. "Read it!" she said. "Go on!"

Alf glanced down at the page.

From: *The Surrey Times*

Within a day of his flat being searched for evidence, Merriweather was charged with the robbery at the Imperial Hotel. Merriweather was taken into custody and transported to Scotland Yard for questioning. Later he found himself at Richmond prison. The trial began on 20 January, at Kingston courthouse before Justice Roderick Coombes.

During proceedings Marcus Baldwin, a forensic detective, took the stand. He testified that the marks found at the scene of the robbery in Kingston and those found at the

Imperial Hotel, Milton Wells, were identical to those made in tests by a claw hammer found in Merriweather's flat.

On 23 March, the jury retired for two days to consider their verdicts. Merriweather was found guilty of robbery and sentenced to fifteen years. He was sent to Wandsworth prison in south London.

Professor Carmichael poured herself a second mug of coffee. "Fifteen years is a long sentence for a crime without violence. I think the police hoped he would own up, tell them where he'd hidden the Pomeranian crown jewels."

"But he didn't?"

"They have never been found. Nor has anything else Percival Merriweather stole."

"And did he stay in prison for fifteen years?"

"I think so," said Professor Carmichael. "And I am absolutely sure he would have eventually made his way back to the place he had hidden everything. He must have known the police or private investigators would have been on his tail. And by the way, here's a copy of the photo of him you saw the other day. I thought you could show it to as many people as possible, see if anyone recognizes him."

"But it's from sixty years ago!" Alf said.

"Doesn't matter, old people have long memories, and you never know, there could be other pictures of him in the strangest places."

She put the tray down on the floor and reached into a briefcase. She slid out a large, glossy photograph of Merriweather, the same one as Alf had seen before, but much bigger, and much sharper.

Alf stared at the man's face. There was something in his eyes that he recognized. He looked like a man who knew he could get the better of everyone.

There was a knock at the door and Hattie appeared.

"Alf," she said, "we need help downstairs. Guests want breakfast."

And then something caught Hattie's attention.

"That's funny," said Hattie. "What's that?" She was pointing to a photograph on the top of a pile.

Professor Carmichael reached across, picked it up and passed it to her. "It's the hammer the Invisible Claw used," she said.

"And this is him," said Alf. "This is the Invisible Claw." He was still staring at the face, still convinced he recognized something.

"What do these words written on the hammer

mean?" asked Hattie. "Three of Gold?"

"I think it was his name for the hammer. Three claws, it helped him strike gold," said the professor. "Strange, isn't it?"

"Sounds a bit like a crossword clue," said Hattie.

"I know those eyes," said Alf. "Remember what you said when you were drawing me, Hattie. Eyes stay the same."

"I've got it!" shrieked Hattie.

"You know who this is?" said Alf, holding out the photo. The professor jumped up.

"No, not that. This photo. Three of Gold. It's an anagram. Shift the letters around and you get. . ."

"What?" said Alf, moving up to her side.

"What?" said the professor, craning her neck to look.

"Easy, rearrange the letters and you get The Old Forge!"

"Of course! That's it!" Alf shouted. "He was here!"

"What?" said the professor.

"What?" said Hattie.

"Percival Merriweather, the Invisible Claw. He was here all the time. He still is!"

Alf rushed out of the door, Hattie and the professor behind him. He flew down the stairs, waving the photograph of Merriweather above his head. "I've got you!" he yelled. "I've got you!"

Two potholers standing in reception stepped to one side when they heard Alf yelling. He skidded to a halt under the framed portrait of Albert and Mary on the steps of the hotel, serene and proud, surrounded by the cooks and servants and gardeners.

Hattie and the professor joined him, one looking over each shoulder. Alf pointed to a figure in the back row.

And there he was, grinning between two chambermaids. It was him. The same moustache, the same expression in the eyes. Percival Merriweather, the Invisible Claw.

"You made me realize it, Hattie. He had it all planned! It was his brilliant scheme to ruin the Imperial. He worked here all the time. The words on the hammer spell out why he really did it! He did it for us, for the Old Forge Hotel!"

TWENTY-THREE

The rain couldn't last for ever. That day the heavy cloud moved away and once again the tree-lined streets of Milton Wells were filled with warm sunshine.

A group of the potholers stood on the steps of the hotel and studied the sky.

"The forecast is good," Alf heard one say. He knew what this meant. They would be leaving soon.

As Cardew and Tom Picton cooked, Alf took orders and whisked plates into the dining room. He took trays of tea and coffee. He ran with racks of hot toast and butter, honey and marmalade.

A big man with a mop of curly hair called him over to his table. Alf recognized him as one of the potholers who had stayed before.

"Alf," he said. "Today's the day."

"What?" said Alf, his eyes scanning the table to see if there was anything he could clear away.

"You and your sister are coming with us. Your dad has agreed. We've asked him."

Alf didn't understand.

The four potholers around the table nodded and smiled. One raised a coffee cup. "To Alf," he said, and without prompting, every other cup in the dining room was raised.

"To Alf!" they cheered.

Alf grinned, felt excited, and then wondered if it was a trick.

Dressed in the oldest clothes they had, two pairs of everything except the helmets they had borrowed, Alf and Hattie set off into the morning air. They were at the head of a line of potholers who marched behind them along the pavement, bags swinging, their voices raised in excitement.

"We've been cooped up for too long," said the big man with the mop of hair. He introduced himself as Phil. "I can't believe you've never been to Mill Hole," he said. "It's on your doorstep!"

"Never had time," said Alf.

"Is it dangerous?" said Hattie.

Phil laughed. "Not compared to a normal day at the Old Forge Hotel!"

The grass was still wet from the rain and Alf soon felt the wet seeping through not just his boots but his two layers of socks. They began to squelch and Alf realized there was a long way to go before he would be taking them off again.

"I hope nothing terrible happens when we're out," Hattie whispered across to Alf.

"What do you mean?"

"Like Mum and Dad sell the hotel. Don't you think we should be there, trying to do something?"

"What more can we do?" said Alf. "We've filled every room in the hotel, and even discovered the identity of the Invisible Claw."

"We could find out where he hid the treasure!" said Hattie. "That would solve all our problems! Is that what the professor's doing now?"

"I think she's gone down to London. She wants to find out where Merriweather went after he was released from prison. If she can find that out, she thinks it may lead us to the crown jewels."

From the back of the line, low voices began to sing in time to the rhythm of their walk. The descent suddenly became steeper, and the path began to cross the slope at an angle.

"Do you know where we are now?" Phil asked. Alf shook his head.

Phil slowed for a moment, and turned back to face the way they had come. He pointed up to the top of the ridge. Alf saw a row of tall white buildings.

"The middle one of those is your hotel," Phil told him. "Don't tell me you don't even recognize your own home!"

"Not ours for long," said Hattie from behind them.

"What does she mean?" Phil asked Alf.

"My mum and dad have to sell up. We'll probably be moving soon."

"Oh," he said. "And by the looks on your faces you're not very happy about that, are you?"

Phil led them down the path as it zigzagged between huge rocks that seemed to have burst out of the soil. Rabbits bounced off ahead of them, and every so often a squirrel shot up a tree trunk.

Alf had just begun to feel the morning sun warming through his clothes when he noticed the temperature drop. Below them a shallow wooded valley lay in the shadow of the hill. And then Alf saw another group of potholers.

"This is it," said Phil. "Mill Hole Pot."

The entrance to the cave was smaller than Alf had expected, and as the other group disappeared inside, Alf watched as the light from their lamps criss-crossed the ceilings and walls until they were gone.

"Patrick is coming with us," said Phil. "We'll lead off, the others will follow. But first, let me give you one of these each. In case you get lost."

Whistles were hung around their necks on a thin cord. Then they were each handed a torch.

"Right then," said Patrick, a man with green

eyes and fiery red eyelashes. "This is a gentle stroll. But it's cold and wet."

They followed Patrick into the darkness and immediately the tunnel twisted sharply to the left, and began to rise.

"We have to climb for a bit," said Phil, his voice reverberating against the wet rock. "Then everything starts to open out."

Occasionally the torches flashed on to a stream that tumbled down the path under their feet. Alf began to feel his socks getting wetter and his feet beginning to rub.

They reached the caverns. Alf looked up into the darkness of the domed ceiling. The rocks here were twisted like rope, and great stalactites hung dangerously way above them. Ahead of them another group swept the wall with torchlight, occasionally resting on a peculiar rock formation. There was one that looked like a witch, another like a unicorn.

"And what you have to understand," said Phil, "is that caves like this, and some much bigger, are everywhere around here. It's like an underground city. Milton Wells on top, another town, like a reflection, down below."

"Are we going to see all the caves?" said Hattie.

"You'd need to wriggle on your belly like a snake through tunnels narrower than a hosepipe," said Phil, laughing. "These are the only ones that amateurs get to see."

They moved across the great cave to a dark opening in a far wall. As Alf stepped through he heard the roar of rushing water.

"If someone bottled this stuff," said Phil, shouting over the noise, "they would make a fortune! It's the most beautiful water in the world."

And then they came to the last cave. At first Alf thought it was far less spectacular than the earlier ones, but when he looked up he realized he was staring into a huge black void. When the torches flickered across the walls he began to sense the scale of the cavern above him. Way above, right at the top, was a tiny disc of light.

"This is Mill Hole Pot," said Phil. "Big enough to fit a hot air balloon inside. I abseiled down it once. And I won't do it again."

"Some nutters scale up the inside," said Patrick. "But you have to be mad to try." Alf couldn't imagine how it would be possible to climb these sheer sides. The walls leant away from the small circle of cave floor where they stood, then tapered dramatically near the top; Alf imagined anyone climbing here would be hanging on by their fingertips.

"OK, come on, then," said Patrick. "Let's go

back to the main cave and have something to eat."

Alf was about to turn away and follow the others back out when his torch picked out something on an overhang of rock high above his head.

Once he had seen it, he saw it again and again. On columns, boulders and the junction into the tunnel. It was everywhere. It even seemed to spiral up the inside of the cave walls. He was sure, absolutely certain, it was same thing. The three short lines cut into stone. The Three of Gold, the mark of the Invisible Claw.

TWENTY-FOUR

Alf and Hattie were so tired at the end of their expedition that Phil and Patrick had to almost push them home. Alf was not just exhausted, his feet were soaked and cold, his toes rubbed raw. He felt sore and miserable.

When they climbed over the stile into the square Alf saw what he thought was a breakdown truck parked alongside the hotel, a cable stretching from its towing crane looping into the lounge window. For a moment he thought someone had come to pull the building down. He could hear Cardew shouting, but couldn't see him: "Try and get it round his belly, get it nice and tight."

Inside, Alf found his father standing in the crater, perspiring and looking flustered. "We've got some gear to try and pull the Buddha out," he explained. Cardew, balanced on a crutch, stood above, a hand gripped around the cable. Hattie and the potholers filed in to look.

"That's not going to work," Phil said immediately. "If that cable snaps it'll take the windows out.

Leave it for now and see we'll see what we can do. We use lifting gear all the time. Professional equipment, not something like this."

"Well, I'm not sure," said Tom Picton. "I've already had to put down a big deposit to hire this lot."

Phil squatted down and put one hand on the Buddha's white head. "We'll do it as a favour. You've been good to us; this hotel has always been our favourite. Let's say we're repaying a debt."

Tom Picton smiled and nodded. Alf could see he was relieved. "That's kind of you," he said. "Let's call it a day. And if you can make it this week, we can get on with sorting out the paperwork for the sale."

Alf and Hattie stared at their father.

"For the sale?" said Alf.

Tom Picton scrambled up out of the hole. He was splattered with wet earth.

"When you were out two men interested in buying the hotel came to see us. They own a group of restaurants. They think the Old Forge is perfect for them. They loved the garden. They made us an offer, there and then. A good offer."

Alf was speechless for a moment. He felt Phil's hand on his shoulder.

"Dad," said Alf. "We filled the hotel. We could do it again. You can't do this. Not now. You promised."

"We have to. We're broke. If we don't pay the money we owe people, we'll be taken to court. If we sell up, we can settle up with everyone and start again."

The sound of a door slamming and footsteps running through the hotel cut the conversation short. Purvis threw back the lounge door and stood there, trying to catch his breath, his eyes wide.

"Tom," he said at last. "You better come and see this. It's awful. Really awful."

"What is it, Purvis?" said Tom Picton. "What's happened now?" He ran his hand over his unshaven face. He wore an expression that suggested he didn't really want to know.

"Just follow me," said Purvis.

All of them trailed after the gardener through the reception, then into the dining room and out on to the terrace. Purvis moved to the edge, then stood there and pointed down. Tom, Alf, Hattie, Cardew and the potholers jostled forward to look.

At first Alf couldn't quite believe what he was seeing. The lawn was a muddy brown swamp. It looked as if the garden had been bombed. Scoops of red-brown earth, like muddy islands, dotted the lawn.

"Molehills," said Cardew.

"Looks like a battlefield," said a potholer.

Alf's father shook his head.

Purvis explained. "When you were struggling with the Buddha, I had to nip out to get parts for the lawnmower. I took a little longer than I'd anticipated. When I got back, this is what I found. All that love and care and attention I've given this lawn. And the moles wreck it in a few hours. And it'll get worse."

Tom Picton sighed. "Just as we get a buyer for the hotel, this happens. They could come back tomorrow for another look. If they see the garden like this, they could call the whole thing off."

"I tell you, Tom," said Purvis, "I know something about moles. They are difficult to shift. It only takes three or four, and they can wreck a life's work."

Alf was more worried about his father than the lawn. Tom Picton stared down at the devastation and kept shaking his head.

"It's bad, isn't it?" said Purvis.

"Do you know anyone who gets rid of moles?" Tom asked at last.

"There's only one person I can think of who can sort it out," said Purvis. "The best mole man in the county. He's a professional and he's ruthless. His name's Rex. He's known as the Terminator. Rex Terminator."

TWENTY-FIVE

The ghost mole appeared to Alf for the third time as he was cleaning boots. The potholers were leaving that morning, but had promised to return soon to pull the Buddha from the lounge floor. Alf wanted to make sure they left with their boots cleaner than when they had arrived.

Forty pairs were lined up along the kitchen wall. Alf placed his watch at one end and began timing. First he scraped off the dried mud, then applied polish, then he brushed, and then he used a rag to make them shine. He wanted the morning sunshine to reflect off their toes.

As he came to the last boot a voice whispered from inside it.

"You have all the facts now, dear boy," said Craddock.

Alf picked up the boot to look inside.

"You know all you need to know."

Alf checked over one shoulder, then the other. He was alone. He didn't want anyone overhearing this. He pushed his fingers into the boot but felt nothing. He peered in, and for a moment thought he saw a puckered nose, and then the glint of a tiny eye.

"Yes," said Alf. "It will be me who solves this, not you. You don't exist."

"But I do, old chap. I exist in your heart. And you know it. I will live in this old hotel for ever. It's my home."

"Are you going to tell me your big secret? Can you tell me anything at all?"

"Just think about it this way. Moles – we dig tunnels. Look for the tunnels, and you find the moles."

"What does that mean?"

"Tunnels, Alf," Craddock's voice seemed as if it was moving into the distance, or echoing from deep within a cave.

"Why do you keep coming back? Why a mole? Why not appear as yourself?"

"I thought I'd explained all that," said Craddock. "I'm one of them now. Well, half of me is. Don't let the moles suffer. Help them out. Find a way of saving the moles, Alf, and then you'll save the hotel. And then I can leave you alone."

"Thank you, Lord Mole," whispered Alf into the boot. "You've just given me an idea."

TWENTY-SIX

"The treasure has to be here somewhere," said Alf. He had spread a map over Hattie's bedroom floor. It was one Phil the potholer had given him as a souvenir. Blue skies filled Hattie's window. The rain had gone. And so had the potholers.

Alf and Hattie studied the map on all fours. The key marked entrances, tunnels, caves and nearby paths and roads.

"Mill Hole Pot," announced Alf, prodding the map with a finger, "that's where I saw the marks of the Three of Gold. Merriweather must have been there."

"But think of all the people who would have been through those tunnels in the last sixty years," Hattie said. "If the crown jewels had been hidden there, they would have been found by now."

Alf sighed. She was right. But then he had another thought. "Perhaps," he said, getting excited again, "Merriweather knew of other, secret passages. Remember, Hattie, he broke into the Imperial Hotel by coming up through the floor.

He must have gone through a tunnel to get there. But, look, there aren't any tunnels marked on the map under the square, or anywhere near the Imperial. But there must be. And I bet that's where he hid the crown jewels. It all makes sense. He discovers a new way through from the Old Forge to the Imperial. He steals the treasure and hides it in a cave, or a tunnel that only he knows about. He leaves it there and disappears, hoping to return one day to take it away."

"Perhaps he's already come and gone," said Hattie. "How would we know?"

"We don't," said Alf, sitting up. "But when the potholers come to get the Buddha out, I'm going to ask them if they think there could be some undiscovered tunnels around here." He stood up and went to the door. "There's nothing to lose, is there?"

Hattie shrugged. "You just don't give up hoping, do you? I'm more worried about those moles. As long as the moles are digging up the lawn, we can't go. Dad has sent for a mole murderer."

Alf swiped up the map by a corner and folded it along a crease. "You look after the moles, Hattie. I'm looking for hidden treasure. I know something will turn up. I just know it will. It has to!"

Pulling the half-folded map behind him like a kite, he left Hattie alone and made his way downstairs. The key to the professor's room was on its hook. She still hadn't returned. He hoped she wouldn't give up.

He placed the map on the desk in reception and continued to fold it, to try to get it back to its original shape, but it wouldn't flatten out. He opened it up and tried again. He began to get frustrated.

"I just can't work this out!" he shouted.

A shadow fell across the desk. Alf looked up.

An enormous man in a motorcycle helmet and a long black beard stood there, staring down at him. His leather jacket creaked as he pulled the goggles off the top of his head.

"I've come to see Mr Picton," he said in a deep growl. "Rex Terminator," he announced, pointing to the ghoulish white insignia on the front of his helmet. "The sign of the mole skull." Then he did a mad wide grin to reveal his teeth; one at the top was gold and bright, two below were sharpened to a point.

"Tyrannosaurus Rex," he snarled. "Mole exterminator."

TWENTY-SEVEN

Tom Picton and Rex stood on the lawn. Several new and bigger molehills had appeared. Rex took a swing at them with his boot, spraying the flower beds with earth.

Purvis and Cardew, who had been sitting outside the greenhouse chatting, stood up.

Alf and Hattie looked down from the terrace. Now that the rain had drained away and the molehills were clearly visible, Alf could see they formed a pattern. From where they stood, the molehills formed an unmistakable giant X.

"Hattie," Alf said at last, "do the molehills spell anything to you?"

"Trouble," Hattie answered. "What are we going to do? He's going to murder all the moles."

"And us probably," said Alf. "Have you seen his teeth?"

"Don't say things like that," said Hattie, shivering.

"This is a mess, Mr Picton," said Rex. "There's a

colony of moldywarps under there. Generations of them."

"How long will it take to get rid of them?" Tom asked.

"Depends," said Rex. "There may be a whole army of them. I might need to use nuclear weapons." He laughed. Tom Picton didn't. "Don't worry, Mr Picton," said Rex, "in twenty-four hours the whole lot of them will be dead."

Rex tramped back through the hotel, Alf and Hattie following him to his big black motorcycle parked outside. He unbuckled one of the large leather saddlebags at the back of the bike and took out a new pair of gardening gloves. Rex saw the children staring down from the top of the steps.

"The moldywarps," he said, tugging on the gloves, "can smell a human from way off. Even the slightest touch of my fingertip and they'll sniff trouble." Then he pulled out two handfuls of tangled metal, dropped them on to the pavement and rebuckled the bag. "See these?" He pointed to the heap of metal. "These are mole traps. They snap the mole's back. It won't feel pain, so don't feel sorry for the poor moldywarp."

Hattie put her hand over her face and ran in. Rex clanked back through the hotel and into the garden.

"You're not going to follow me around like this all day, are you?" growled Rex, as Alf crept behind him. "Because you're making me nervous."

Alf stopped and turned. He ran upstairs to find Hattie, who was lying on her bed, face down, crying.

"He mustn't kill them. What do we do? I hate this! I hate it!"

"I don't know," said Alf. "I don't want him to kill them either. We have to find a way to convince Dad it's worth hanging on for a little longer."

"But we've tried everything," cried Hattie.

Alf hurtled down to reception, grabbed the key to the professor's room, and rushed back up. The place was still a mess, but he found what he was looking for.

He ran back down to find his father. Tom Picton was whistling, gluing the neck of a violin. Alf had never seen him look so serene.

"Dad." Alf was still trying to catch his breath after plummeting down the stairs. "Dad, you mustn't let Rex kill the moles. And you mustn't sell the hotel. Look." He held up the big glossy photo of Percival Merriweather.

"Who is that?" said Dad. "Did you tell me? Someone famous?"

"Please come with me," said Alf. "Just for a few minutes."

Dad sighed, and, still holding the violin neck and a tube of glue, followed Alf through to reception. Alf pointed to the framed photograph on the wall.

"You know, Dad, I've always wondered how Albert and Mary won the cup. And now I know."

Dad's brow furrowed slightly. "Go on," he said.

"This man is Percival Merriweather," said Alf, shaking the photo in his hand. "And look, here he is on the steps of the Old Forge, at the back. He was also known as the Invisible Claw. He robbed the Imperial Hotel, made off with a huge hoard, including, famously, the Pomeranian crown jewels."

Dad's mouth had dropped open.

"I am pretty sure he was a potholer, maybe one of the first to explore the tunnels around here. He may even have come to Milton Wells because of the caves, I don't know. But he discovered a way to get into the Imperial. He broke into the strongroom, through the floor, and helped himself to their valuables. Because no one knew how he had done it, the guests in the Imperial got scared. And what did they do? They fled across the square to here. What they didn't know, of course, was that the Invisible Claw was here. By the look of him, I'd guess he was one of the gardeners. He was arrested in London a few years after the burglary.

He used a three-clawed hammer – very unusual. It's how they got him. And this is it." He produced the photo of the hammer. "Do you see what's written on it?"

Tom Picton furrowed his brow and glanced up at Alf. "Three of Gold?"

"Yes, Dad," said Alf. "It's an anagram. Move the letters around. You know what you get? The Old Forge! It's some sort of message, Dad, to himself, or to the future! But he was doing this for the hotel, I am sure of that."

"How do you know all this?"

"The professor and me, we've been doing a little detective work. The thing is, Dad, the Pomeranian crown jewels were never found. And Pomerania doesn't exist any more. The king and queen were here because they had fled their country. There was a revolution. They were kicked out. The jewels could be hidden here, Dad, somewhere in the hotel. If we find them, we could claim them. You'd have some money to pay off the bills. We could stay."

Mr Picton didn't know what to say. He looked from Alf to the photograph on the wall and back to Alf.

"You're making this up," he said. "Aren't you?"

"No, ask the professor. She'll be back soon. She's gone to London to try and find out where

Merriweather went after he had served his sentence. He got fifteen years. They hoped he'd own up, reveal where the jewels were hidden. But he didn't. I think they could be here, Dad."

"You're dreaming," said Dad. "It's a fantasy. It's ridiculous. The whole story. You just can't accept that we're finished here. I'm sorry, Alf. I know you want to stay. But we can't. If the jewels were hidden here, we would have found them by now."

"Well, I'm still going to look," said Alf. "They're here somewhere, Dad. They have to be."

TWENTY-EIGHT

"I didn't like the look of him," said Cardew, after Rex had gone. "And his beard was bigger than mine."

"He's sunk at least ten traps in there," said Purvis, shaking his head. "He's done more damage than the moles." They stood in a line looking down at the scarred lawn.

"If Rex gets the moles," said Alf, "the hotel is sold. It's all over for us. And for you." Alf saw Purvis narrow his eyes, thinking this through. "Now help me pull the traps out." He took a step on to the lawn.

"You can't do that," said Purvis. "They're in too deep. You'll have to dig them up. And Rex will find out. Your father won't like it. And nor will I. There's a plague of moldywarps here. It's them or the lawn," said Purvis. "Them or us."

"No, it isn't," said Alf. "Kill the moles, the hotel is sold. Are the new owners going to employ you? They have restaurants and hotels all over the place, probably use the same team of gardeners. If they buy the hotel, you are out of a job. It's them or us."

Alf heard a tapping from an upstairs window. He turned to see Professor Carmichael waving down at him.

"She's back!" he cried and raced into the hotel, Hattie behind him.

The professor was eager to tell Alf her news but couldn't get a word in. Alf couldn't stop talking. Without taking a breath he told her about his discovery in the caves; how it had suddenly occurred to him that the Invisible Claw must have been here all the time; how Merriweather could have found a tunnel or a cave that ran under the Imperial.

"Brilliant!" gasped the professor, nodding furiously at Alf's explanation. "Marvellous!" she said. "Incredible!" And, "Ingenious!"

Alf sat down on the end of her bed and tried to catch his breath.

"And what did you find out in London, Professor?" asked Hattie, sitting down next to her brother.

"I discovered a private detective, very old, and retired. He was in his late eighties. For many years he had tried to help the king of Pomerania recover the crown jewels. Fifteen years after the jewels were stolen the king was living somewhere in

England. His country didn't want him back, and in a few years it wouldn't exist anyway. This old detective, Ray Sims, he followed Merriweather after his release from prison. There was no doubt Merriweather had made some money from the smaller valuables he had stolen from the Imperial, but the crown jewels were still missing." The professor was so excited her hands were clenched into fists. She was shaking them together as she spoke, eager to let them know everything as quickly as possible.

"Now listen, you two," she went on. "Sims followed Merriweather to Wornham. He rented a flat there, and found a job as a park keeper. And now and then, on the occasional weekend, he would pay a visit to Milton Wells. And just as you said, he was a potholer. Sims told me he would follow Merriweather to cave entrances, and he would wait until he reappeared. Sims was hoping Merriweather would appear with the jewels, but it didn't happen."

"So the jewels are definitely still missing?" Alf asked.

"Yes, and Sims thinks they are here somewhere, in a cave, perhaps, or underground. But eventually the king ran out of money and decided he couldn't afford to keep paying Sims, so that was that."

Alf shrugged and looked disappointed. He didn't mean to, but he couldn't help it. The professor had only confirmed his story.

"We're nowhere nearer to finding the jewels, are we?" said Alf. "And if we don't, we're finished, it's all over; we're going to have to leave. I can just imagine the new owners discovering them within a few weeks of being here." Alf sighed. "You know about Rex Terminator, I suppose?"

"Yes, I met your father on the way in. He told me what was going on. But," said the professor, "I haven't finished telling you my story. I looked in the Wornham Parks and Gardens offices for records of their employees. Merriweather worked there for five years. So, twenty years after stealing the crown jewels, he left Wornham. And the astonishing thing is, he completely disappears. There's no record of him working in Wornham, or living there. There are census records, street directories, all these things that you can use to trace people. He's gone. So where did he go?"

"Back to London?" suggested Alf.

"But he had come here to recover the jewels, I'm sure of that. Perhaps he did find them, and emigrated, or something like that. But just before I left, Sims he said something that made me wonder."

"What?" Alf was hoping this might be the

breakthrough. If the professor didn't offer some hope now, there was nothing left for him to do but give up.

"Sims said that Merriweather was beginning to change his appearance, smarten himself up. He began wearing suits in the evening. He joined a gentlemen's club in Wornham, a place for local businessmen. No women: they weren't allowed in!"

"What was he up to?" said Alf.

"I am sure he was going to change his identity. He was learning how to be a gentleman. He was going to become someone else."

"Could he still be alive?" The thought had never occurred to Alf before.

"Well, Percival Merriweather has certainly disappeared into thin air. If he is alive now he probably uses another name. And he would be a very old man indeed. Sims, the private detective, would be about the same age."

Alf sat silently for a while, imagining what Merriweather would look like now.

"He could be here," said the professor. "In Milton Wells. A very rich man!" She lowered her voice. "But, Alf, I know the address of the gentlemen's club in Wornham. Tomorrow morning, I'm taking the bus there. You never know, perhaps I'll find out where Mr Merriweather is now!" The professor stood up and walked across the room. She looked down into the garden. "What are those two doing?" she said, opening the window. Alf and Hattie squeezed up next to her.

Cardew was shuffling across the damaged lawn, dragging his plaster cast across the grass. Here and there he poured something from a jug. Purvis looked on, grinning.

"What's going on?" yelled Alf.

Cardew raised the jug. "The wonder of Welsh wee!" he declared, chuckling. He continued on, bobbing across the lawn, a trickle here, a splash there.

Purvis looked up. "You saw Rex was wearing those new gloves," he shouted. "It's because he didn't want to touch the traps with his hands. One sniff of a human and the moles smell danger."

Cardew straightened up again. "We can't pull the traps up, because they'll bite our fingers off. So I did a mighty wee in this jug, you see. And now I'm pouring it over the places where Rex buried the traps. The moles won't like the whiff of my widdle and they won't go near the traps now! Rex won't have a clue what's happened!"

The professor began to laugh.

"Sniff this, moleys!" shouted Cardew, his words

breaking into a cackling laugh. "Rex Terminator may have the weapons, but we have the widdle!"

"The moles live to fight another day," said the professor.

"And so does the Old Forge Hotel!" Alf grinned.

TWENTY-NINE

Alf was dressing quickly. He wanted to be downstairs to watch the Buddha being dragged from the crater. He caught his fingers on the inside of his jacket, there was a tearing sound and the sleeve came away. For a few moments, he stood in his room, staring at the limp tube of cloth, wondering what to do with it. But there was quite a bit of noise coming from downstairs. The potholers were here. He threw the sleeve on the bed and went to see what was going on.

"Here's Alf!" bellowed one of the potholers. They were all there, waiting in reception. They cheered and greeted him with waves and smiles.

Phil approached Alf and winked. "We're going to get the Buddha out," he said. "Then we'll try and take it on to the terrace. It'll be safer there."

"I'll get the kettle on, then," said Alf. He ferried mugs of tea through to the lounge and was watching the winch being brought in when he heard the unmistakable sound of a motorbike pulling up outside. The mole man was back.

Rex strode through the hotel and out into the garden as if he owned the place. Alf scurried behind him.

"Good morning, gentlemen," said Rex. Purvis and Cardew were working on the vegetable patch. They looked at each other, Cardew winked, and they made their way towards the lawn.

Rex dropped a canvas bag on to the grass. Alf noticed Rex's shadow fall across the lawn, a stunted twin. It was like death itself walked alongside him.

"Let's see how many moldywarps Rex has terminated," said the mole man.

The leather-clad giant stood over a point in the lawn where the first trap was buried. He took a shovel from his bag and began scraping away loose soil. Then he thrust a metal hook into the ground, and drew it out again. Once more, he rammed it down, turned it, and seemed to be listening for something. The third time he nodded and began to rummage with his fingers.

"Sounds like this one has been sprung. Let's see, shall we?"

He reached down, easing the trap out of the ground. His finger was hooked through a metal loop at the top of the contraption. And when he stood with it, and held it out before everyone, it was like he'd just caught a big, ugly fish.

For just a second or two, Rex looked bewildered.

Then the jaws clanged and the trap almost leapt from his hands. Rex jerked backwards, Alf cowered, and Purvis and Cardew, some distance away, jumped in surprise.

The trap was empty. Rex had assumed it had been triggered, but it hadn't. He was even more dangerous now; he had been humiliated before an audience. They had seen the expert not only make a mistake; they had seen him flinch.

When he moved to the second trap Rex dug the hook into the ground six times until it snapped shut. Then, without looking up from his task, or making a sound, he triggered each device before pulling it up empty. Each one he flung down with greater force. Not one of the traps had been set off. His score was zero. He hadn't caught a single mole.

Rex stared down at the empty traps and said nothing. Then he gathered them up and threw them, along with his tools, into his bag and zipped it. He drew himself up to his full height, his fists clenched, his eyes burning. He looked like a beast about to spring. He twisted slowly and glared at each spectator in turn. When he spoke next, his voice had changed. It was now a deeper, rumbling growl.

"Who did this?" he snarled. "Who did this?"

Cardew put his hand to his beard. Purvis raised his eyebrows and shrugged. Alf knew his turn was coming, and when the monster's eyes met his, he didn't look away.

Then Rex grimaced, baring his teeth. He pulled down the goggles over his eyes. "I have never failed," he said. "I curse this place," he spat. "But I'm not beaten yet. I'll get those moles. Even if I have to rip out the whole lawn, I'll get them!" And with that he strode out of the garden and through the hotel. They heard his motorbike start up and knew he had gone.

Cardew and Purvis grabbed each other and began dancing in a loping circle. They spun round and round and then fell over, bursting into giggles as they sprawled on the mud-caked lawn.

Alf laughed and ran back through to the lounge to see if the winch was in place.

"You'd be surprised how often we need to use this," said Phil, patting one of the metal supports. "We've fished out all sorts of things from holes in the ground. Tractors, a horse, cattle, a caravan. Never a Buddha, though. This is a first."

The gang worked as a team, as if they had done so many times before. Two were in the hole, three worked at setting up the winch. A few others stood around joking; Alf realized this meant it looked an easy job, that the Buddha would soon be pulled free.

"The hardest part will be getting it outside," said Phil. "That's why there are so many of us. Don't need that many usually."

Hattie came in when the lifting began.

"I missed the mole man," she said to Alf. "Why didn't you tell me?"

"Too much going on," said Alf. "The moles are safe for the moment." He grinned. "By the wonder of Welsh widdle. Now let's see if we can rescue the Buddha."

The winch squeaked, then roared, the cable went tight and soon the Buddha began to appear. Three men stood next to it and held it away from the edge of the hole as it emerged. Two brave potholers stood in the crater, making sure nothing obstructed its ascent.

It surfaced like a mysterious white sea creature, one that had been hidden from sunlight and human eyes for hundreds of years. The ropes and cables wound around it like seaweed, but the Buddha looked tranquil and unconcerned.

When the statue was fully out, the whole apparatus swivelled elegantly to lower it gently on to a trolley, ready to be wheeled away.

A shout came from within the crater. "Hey! Look what we've got here!"

The gang began to shuffle forward and gather around the hole. Alf and Hattie squeezed through the bodies, and found themselves looking down at two potholers in the pit. One of them Alf recognized as Patrick.

"What is it?" asked Phil.

Below the line of the broken floorboards there was a second, older floor, then snapped wooden joists. The crater was a hollow of dark red soil, but just behind the two men a large shoulder of rock, about Alf's height, protruded from the mud. In the middle of this, and just above the level of the water in the bottom of the crater, there was a large dark hole.

"Has anyone brought a torch?" asked Patrick.

Three arms shot out, each offering identical torches. One was passed down. Patrick squatted next to the hole and shone the torch inside.

"Gentlemen," he said in a very measured voice. "I think we have made something of a discovery." And then he took a breath and yelled, "Hello!" and everyone heard the echo.

"A cave," said Patrick. "And it sounds like a very big one!"

There was a little jostling as each of the cavers pushed towards the edge of the crater, eager to climb down and have a look for themselves. Then, donning helmets and grabbing odd pieces of kit, one by one they disappeared into the hole, their voices raised. Alf listened as their shouts were lost in the depths of the newly discovered world.

Phil told Alf and Hattie to stay where they were until he came back. They sat down on the edge of the crater, swinging their legs. Phil ducked down and disappeared into darkness.

"I don't know what's so interesting about caves, do you?" said Hattie. "They're dark, wet, cold and smelly places. You can stay here if you like. I'm going to see if I can stop anyone else from having a go at the moles."

"What?" said Alf. "How?"

"I've thought of a little plan," she said, smiling. She stood up, grinned at him, and went off.

He wasn't waiting alone for long. Phil pushed up out of the crater, damp and muddy, his face pink with exuberance.

He clambered out, rummaged through one of the backpacks and pulled out a caving helmet, which he placed on Alf's head.

"I crown you king of Picton Hole." He slipped back into the crater. "And now, Your Majesty, please come with me."

Alf squeezed through the hole, then wriggled behind Phil along the low tunnel, until they came to a ledge. Phil guided him on to a rope ladder and Alf began to descend. As his hands grew cold the rungs became more and more difficult to feel. Torches swept the damp air. Excited chatter echoed around the chamber and there was the occasional burst of nervous laughter.

Alf stepped down on to the cave floor and gasped. The cave was enormous, a cathedral of bright stone. Natural columns twisted like vines to the dome above; on the far side a waterfall leapt from an overhanging rock and fell into a pool below.

Phil shone his torch back the way they had come. At the foot of the rope ladder were a series of openings.

"Look," he said. "There are other entrances to this cave. There must be tunnels running deep under your hotel and probably leading back to Mill Hole."

Alf wondered if this was how Percival Merriweather found his way into the cave. He couldn't possibly have come through the lounge floor. And was the treasure here somewhere? Alf squinted into the darkness, and as the torches illuminated one possible hiding place after another, he hoped for a sudden glint of a jewel.

Further on, a series of elaborate natural arches suggested another domain beyond. Phil gestured for them to follow. The other cavers were waiting for them there. Once they stepped between the columns, they found themselves inside a hollow cylinder of rock that towered up above them.

"It's a natural chimney," said Phil, his light tracing a spiral up the inside. "And the ceiling here is much higher than in the other cave. Even these powerful torches can't penetrate up there."

Sure enough, when the beams were raised, they were swallowed up in darkness.

"It's so high," said Phil, "that I imagine there can be very little between the top of the cave and the surface."

And then Alf saw the marks in the stone. They started just above the level of his head and wound up the inside of the chimney: three claw marks.

"Yes," said Phil, "someone has been here before us. And as far as I can see, he has gone all the way up."

"The Imperial Hotel," said Alf. He just knew. "It's right above our heads."

"It better not be," said Phil.

"I'm certain it is," said Alf. "Those marks, they are the work of the Invisible Claw, Percival Merriweather. He must have used these caves to get into the Imperial."

Phil shouted over to the others. "Alf here reckons the Imperial Hotel is above us. What do you think?"

"Well, if it is, it's lucky it hasn't fallen straight

through," said Patrick. "This chimney goes all the way up. Anything built over it can't be safe."

Alf looked at him.

Phil leant forward to try and explain. "The Imperial Hotel is floating on a ceiling of rock not much thicker than a paving stone."

"Wouldn't want to stay there," said Patrick. "It could fall through at any moment."

Phil cleared his throat. "Well, then, I think it's our duty to inform the authorities. Before the ground gives way beneath it."

Percival Merriweather might still keep the secret of his treasure, but once again, just as had happened in the month of the Claw all those years ago, the Imperial Hotel was about to get a nasty surprise.

THIRTY

Alf hadn't expected things to happen so fast.

A grim-faced safety inspector arrived in a dusty yellow van.

Phil took him into the caves. Fifteen minutes later, the inspector was on the phone, his forehead furrowed in concern. Alf was surprised the police were involved, but when the patrol car turned into the square, its blue light flashing, he began to realize this was extremely serious.

Jobson watched from the steps of the Imperial as the police jumped out of the car and ran past him into the hotel, not waiting for him to even raise his hat, never mind reach out for the door.

Minutes later staff and guests were being evacuated. They gathered on the pavement, bewildered and angry, and were quickly ushered across the road to gather around the statue of Saint Barlow. A large white truck rumbled into the square and stopped behind the police car. A man stepped out and opened up the van's rear doors. He pulled out a large triangular sign from his vehicle. It read: "DANGER UNSAFE BUILDING". Then he began putting a barrier of bollards and bright tape around the hotel.

Some of the evicted guests sat down on the benches under the sun-dappled statue of Saint Barlow. Others stood next to their suitcases and watched the events that followed.

The manager, staff and few remaining guests were ushered from the hotel by the two policemen. The last to be escorted from the building was Norman Jobson. He had a policeman at each arm, and Alf could hear his protests from the other side of the square.

Alf made his way across the road and towards the statue. Two middle-aged men were standing by their suitcases, quietly debating what to do.

One looked at his watch. "We could still catch a train," Alf heard one say.

"I was looking forward to these few days," said the other.

"What's going on?" said Alf.

Both men stared at him, then looked back at each other.

"Why is everyone being asked to leave?" asked Alf. He knew, of course, but wanted to hear it from one of the guests.

"The police say the hotel isn't safe. They have

information that leads them to believe it could collapse at any moment."

"That's terrible," said Alf.

"And it was the first day of the conference," said one of the men.

"What conference?" Alf asked, innocently.

"Accountants," the man replied.

"Plenty of room at the Old Forge," said Alf. "And I'm sure we could try and run the conference there."

"Really?" said the second man, his face breaking into a smile. He picked up his suitcase. "I'll just tell the others."

Alf ran back to the hotel. He bounded up the steps, crashed through the main door and into reception.

"Hello!" he yelled, but no answer came. They would be here soon, the guests from the Imperial; he needed to tell everyone, now, as soon as possible. Where were they? Then he remembered the last thing Hattie had said to him. Her plan. What was it?

He ran through the kitchen and pulled open the door to the garden. And there was Hattie. Her mouth hung open; she looked dazed.

"Hattie?" said Alf.

She closed her mouth, then opened it again to speak, but made no sound.

"Hattie?" he said again. "What's happened?"

Hattie reached out, took his hand and gently led him across the garden.

Purvis and Cardew were standing on the lawn, a bucket on the ground between them. Spades lay discarded, soil scattered everywhere.

There were huge holes in the dark earth.

"I was just coming to find you," said Hattie at last. "We rescued the moles. I wanted to make sure no one else had a chance to hurt them."

Purvis pointed into the bucket. "Four of them," he said. "Four can do a lot of damage. We think that's all of them."

Alf peered into the bucket. There they were, small velvet creatures with huge ungainly claws, and noses snuffling the air. All still alive.

"But then, just as we were about to stop, we saw this." She pointed into a deep hole. There was something sticking out at an angle. "I wanted you to be here when we pulled it out," she said. Alf could hear her voice trembling. "You remember we saw the molehills from the professor's window? They made a big letter X."

Alf dropped on to his hands and knees and began scraping at the object, clearing away loose soil.

And then he started to shake. He felt cold, and then hot, and then sick. He knelt at the hole for a moment. Hattie crouched down next to him.

"There," said Alf. "Look."

"It's some sort of chest," said Purvis.

Alf took a deep breath.

"The treasure," he said. "It's the treasure!"

THIRTY-ONE

The chest was smaller than Alf had imagined. He carried it to the greenhouse and lowered it on to a bench. He pulled off the larger clumps of damp soil from the dark leather hide. Two tan straps buckled the lid to the body of the chest; there was no padlock.

"Is it really treasure?" Hattie said, almost squeaking with excitement. Alf smoothed the last lumps of soil from the dark wood, revealing brass studs.

"Open it," said Cardew. "Let's have a look."

Purvis put a hand on Alf's arm. "Open it, Alf," he said firmly. "It's probably just a load of old junk."

Alf looked at Hattie. He didn't want to undo the buckles; too much hope lay inside. He knew there was something in there, he could tell by its weight. But it could be worthless, someone's keepsakes, nothing more.

He pushed at the first strap; the damp had eaten into it, and the leather felt as if it could crumble in his fingers. Then it slipped through the buckle and flipped out. The second strap didn't want to come at first, it was tighter; the pin was rusted.

"Shall I slice through it?" said Cardew, pulling a penknife from his pocket.

"No, don't, it's coming," said Alf, and after working at the strap for a while longer, he was able to yank it free.

Alf clasped the lid of the chest at each corner. He didn't want to open it. He closed his eyes; he knew this was the moment when all their hopes and dreams could be whisked away, into the evening air.

Hattie leant forward and wrenched it open. Alf heard the gasps around him and looked down.

He could not believe what he saw. Sunlight gleamed on gold. The flashing geometry of precious stones sparked bright spangles around the glass of the greenhouse. Alf saw a crown studded with blue and green stones. There were goblets, gold plates, all of them draped in a tangle of necklaces, pearls and bracelets.

"Well, you two," he heard Cardew say, "I think you've hit the jackpot."

Alf turned and looked at the others. Was it true? Was this happening?

The dazzling, dancing reflections in their eyes told him he wasn't dreaming. It was real.

His hands shook so much he couldn't close the lid. Purvis reached forward and lowered it for him. Alf picked up the chest, wrapped his arms around it and looked from face to face.

"We have to show the others," he said, his voice wavering. "Must show them." He began to run and could hear the others behind him. "We found it!" he yelled. He ran through the kitchen and into the reception. "We've found it! Mum! Dad! Look! Look!"

The hotel's reception was crowded with guests. They were squashed together, only their luggage separating them. Alf's loud cries silenced their soft chatter and they all turned to look at the scruffy gang.

Tom Picton was behind the desk desperately trying to allocate everyone to their rooms as quickly as possible. But now, like everyone else, he was looking at Alf.

Alf's mother, a pile of bed linen in her hands, appeared at the top of the stairs.

Then Alf saw the professor, and Max and Tilda.

"The Pomeranian crown jewels," he said. "We've found them."

"Alf?" his mother said. "Alf?" It was all she could say.

"The lawn's a bit of a mess," said Alf, eventually.

"We rescued some moles," said Hattie. She hadn't realized until then that she was still holding the bucket.

"You have been busy," said the professor.

"Are we rich?" said Hattie.

"Yes," said the professor, "I think you probably are."

THIRTY-TWO

For the next few days, life at the Old Forge went into a spin. Alf felt giddy with disbelief.

Newspaper journalists flooded through the hotel, their cameras popping and snapping. They stamped through to the garden, where Alf and Hattie stood on the lawn, cradling the chest between them in their arms, dazzled and blinking, grinning this way and then that way, answering shouted questions. The others stood behind Alf, hands clasped together, as proud as parents of a newborn baby.

"Ladies and gentlemen," Alf announced, "the story of how this treasure came to be buried in the gardens of the Old Forge Hotel will be told in *The Invisible Claw*, Professor Helena Carmichael's new book. I'm sure you'll be able to speak to her about that soon."

Professor Carmichael knew it was vital to check that the king of Pomerania had no descendants who were able to make a genuine claim on the crown jewels. Was there an heir to the Pomeranian fortune? Did the treasure belong to the hotel? She had her face glued to the phone, and had written letter upon letter and filled in applications to view old documents.

But she didn't seem to be getting anywhere.

The For Sale sign came down, at least for now. Alf's father contacted the people who had shown an interest in buying the hotel, and explained the situation. He left a message for Rex the mole terminator informing him that all the moles had been caught using only the most humane and ingenious methods. His services were no longer required.

The professor took the jewels to the museum, where they were photographed, and from there they were locked up securely in a bank vault in Wornham.

Cardew and Purvis began returfing the lawn.

And when the commotion had begun to die down, Alf and Hattie took the bucket of moles into the woods and set them free. The sun was setting, and the trees on the top of the hill were silhouetted against a crimson sky.

Alf held the torch as Hattie reached into the bucket to coax each little velvet-suited creature into her hand, and from there to be released into the undergrowth.

"That's the four of them," she said. There was

relief in her voice. She had saved them; her mission was complete.

Alf's torch flashed in the bucket. "No, Hattie, there's one more," he said.

"Funny," she replied. "I was sure there were only four."

Alf lifted the last one out, and as he was about to pass it to her, it seemed to look up at him, salute with one of its huge claws, and then wink.

"Brilliant job, General Alf, General Hattie. Congratulations," it said.

"You know, Alf," said Hattie, smiling, "you sounded just like Lord Craddock when you said that."

And later that week, as guests were filing into the dining room for the evening meal, Professor Carmichael came down the stairs. Alf was sitting at the desk in reception staring at the photo of his ancestors.

"I still don't understand why Merriweather left the jewels here," said the professor. "It doesn't make any sense. Did I tell you about my last trip to Wornham?"

Alf shook his head.

"Merriweather joined the gentlemen's club there; it wasn't open to everyone, membership was expensive. My guess is he sold a few of the jewels he stole from wealthier guests to buy himself some new suits, and to afford membership in the club. I am sure he set about creating a new identity for himself. After that, he disappears without trace."

"No other mention of him anywhere?" asked Alf.

"Well, only his name on a board that displays competition winners. It goes back years and years."

"Competition?" said Alf. "What sort of competition?"

The professor thought for a moment. "I think he won the club's snooker tournament once or twice," she said.

Alf felt his legs go weak and reached out to put his hand on the wall for support.

"Alf," said the professor. "Are you all right?"

He couldn't believe that it was true, but after all that had happened in the last few days, anything was possible. He took a few gulps of air, and then stared up at the professor.

"Do you remember," he said, "what I told you Lord Mole had said to me?"

The professor shook her head. "What?" she said, impatiently. "What did he say?"

"He told me to 'look on the cup'," said Alf.

The professor frowned. She didn't understand.

"I did look on the cup," she said. "There was nothing there, nothing."

"But you looked on the wrong cup," said Alf. He nodded up at the photograph of Albert and Mary. "He didn't mean that cup, he meant another one."

"Which one? What other cup is there?" Alf could see the professor was looking annoyed now, as if she was being teased.

Alf smiled. "The cup you won in the croquet competition."

The professor looked stunned. "But I gave that back to you," she said.

"I know," said Alf. "It's just there, sitting on the shelf behind the desk. Shall I go and get it?"

As soon as he looked at the little silver cup, he knew he was right. "I remember Lord Craddock's words," said Alf, "just before I made the presentation to you at the croquet tournament. The prize was just going to be a free weekend at the hotel. But at the last minute he pushed this cup into my hands for me to present as well. He said it was something he had won at snooker."

The professor looked bewildered.

Alf passed her the cup. "His name's on it," he told her. "It isn't very clear, but I must have seen it, and not realized."

Etched neatly, but in tiny letters, across the

middle of the little silver cup, were the words "Percival Merriweather – Club Snooker Champion".

Alf shook his head. He couldn't believe it was true. But it had to be. Lord Craddock and Percival Merriweather were the same person.

"He was here, all the time," said Alf. "In the hotel, in the photograph. His face has changed, but those eyes, I can see them now, the same eyes."

"A potholing enthusiast in his spare time," said Professor Carmichael. "He must have found a tunnel that led to the cave under the Imperial."

"He broke into the Imperial from underneath, stole the jewels, and hid them here," said Alf. "But why didn't he sell them?"

"He couldn't," said the professor. "He knew he was being watched. He must have moved to London, and was prepared to wait until all the fuss had died down."

"But then he was arrested," said Alf. "The hammer gave him away. He spent fifteen years in prison, and even then he had a private detective following him. So he changed his identity. He became Lord Craddock. He changed his appearance, his hairstyle, the way he dressed, the way he spoke. He invented a whole new life story for himself. And then he became a guest at the

Old Forge, and lived here until he ran out of money. Perhaps he was waiting for the moment he thought it was safe to dig up the garden and sell the treasure. But why didn't he just dig it up and go? Why did he stay?"

"He was an old man," said the professor. "Where would he go? He had made a home here, and that could have been all he wanted. Perhaps he meant to tell you about the treasure, but was frightened what would happen if he did."

Alf nodded. "It does make sense, I suppose."

"And remember," said the professor, "everything you learnt from the ghost of Lord Craddock, you probably already knew. You had seen his name on the cup; perhaps, deep down, you even recognized it was him, but didn't want to admit it to yourself. Lord Craddock, someone you loved and trusted, had actually been deceiving you."

"He was the Invisible Claw," said Alf. "What a man."

THIRTY-THREE

There was one last shock.

Alf was carrying luggage to a waiting taxi, seeing guests off, when he saw Joe Grey, the postman, waddling towards him along the pavement. Joe held out a bundle of letters.

"Should I be giving these to you?" he said.

"I won't hide them again, promise," said Alf.

"And there's a special delivery that needs a signature," said Joe.

"Shall I get my dad?" asked Alf.

"It's not for your dad," said the postman. "It's for a Professor Carmichael."

Alf ran up to her room. She had obviously been up early writing her book. She looked lost in her thoughts.

"What can this important letter be?" she said as Alf led her downstairs.

She scribbled a signature for the postman and took the envelope. Joe Grey waddled off.

Alf trotted back up into the hotel, expecting the professor to follow. But she didn't. Ten minutes later she was still standing outside on the steps.

Alf crept back to the main entrance and looked at her through the glass.

She was staring at the letter. There was no movement on her face. Alf pushed open the door and called out to her.

"Professor?"

She didn't look up.

"Professor?"

She blinked, and, turning towards Alf, seemed to be searching for what to say.

"Professor, are you all right?"

"Yes, yes, thank you, Alf. Listen. I think I need to speak to your father and mother alone." She paused for a moment and again glanced down at the letter. "No, perhaps you and Hattie should be there too."

"Now?" said Alf.

"Yes, now, Alf. If there's no one in there, perhaps we could meet in the lounge."

Work still hadn't finished. The room was undergoing some quite drastic renovations, but at least it was clear of dust and debris. The far end of the room was to incorporate a visitors' centre. Wooden railings surrounded the space where the Buddha once sat and a stairway was under construction to allow guests, or paying visitors, to explore the caves.

Alf, Hattie and their mother and father sat together on the old sofa pushed up against the wall at the opposite end of the room.

"What's this all about, Alf?" said Dad, sitting forward, his hands clasped together nervously. "There's quite a bit to do around the place at the moment."

Alf shrugged and shook his head.

Mum sat back and folded her arms. "It has been so busy! I hope we'll be able to employ someone else soon, so I can get back to my college course."

The professor pushed through the door. She gripped the letter in one hand, and a large sheet of paper in the other. Alf was astonished to see she was now dressed in a suit, her hair tied up quite severely. She looked as she did the first time they had met.

He noticed her eyes weren't settling upon them, but darting across the room, glancing at the letter, the sheet of paper, to the floor, the ceiling, anywhere but on the eyes of her small audience.

"Tom, Sarah," she began, and Alf noticed her voice was a different pitch, and trembling. "As you know, I've been making some inquiries into who may be the rightful owner of the crown jewels. Although I had assumed they were yours, you can never be too sure. And even if they weren't, it's likely the legal owners, once tracked down, would be generous, offering a substantial reward. And you can sell your story, of course, the papers will pay. . ." She trailed off and took a deep breath. "I made contact with a firm of solicitors who are good at getting to the bottom of matters like this. I've used them before."

Alf heard his father stifle a sigh. He was getting impatient.

"Well, they have discovered something." The professor began blinking rapidly, as if holding back tears.

"What is it?" said Alf's mum. "Is it bad news?"

"If you don't mind," said the professor, "I need to tell you a story. It won't take long. You'll understand, however, how important it is at the end."

She glanced nervously at the letter in the one hand, then at the paper in the other. At last her eyes settled upon the family.

"Many years ago, when the people of Pomerania began to turn against their king, it was quite clear the royal family was finished. The king, his wife and their young son fled the country. The king wanted a new life with his family, and never to think of Pomerania again. But his brother thought he could win the people round, so the king made some sort of agreement with him, and left."

"But he was still king when he came to Milton Wells, wasn't he?" said Alf.

"Wait a minute. Please, just listen." The professor took a deep breath. "The king's brother was Prince Ludwig. It was Ludwig who stayed in the Imperial Hotel. When he came here he called himself king, but it seems that in truth, he wasn't. As far as the law stands, his elder brother still was. The one who had left a few months before him."

Together, the Picton family sat up. "So what happened to Ludwig's elder brother? Where did he go?"

The professor began to blink wildly. "King Albrecht left Pomerania for England. He changed his name. He became. . ."

Alf saw what was coming. He felt it flying towards him like a bullet.

"Albert!" he shouted.

"Yes," said the professor. "Your great-grandfather was the King of Pomerania!"

"What?" Tom Picton cried. "I never knew my grandfather; he died before I was born. But I can't believe my father wasn't told."

"I don't think Albert wanted anyone to know," said the professor. "Albert wanted to start a new life. He became Albert Picton, probably because he thought it sounded like a good English name. He had a little money, he bought the hotel, he hired staff. He was, by all accounts, a wonderful man whom everybody loved – not least, I expect, Percival Merriweather. But when things in Pomerania got so bad even his brother could not stay there, Ludwig came to England too."

"Why didn't he stay at the Old Forge?" said Hattie. "Why did he go to the Imperial?"

Alf realized his sister still hadn't understood what was coming. Did it matter where Ludwig stayed? He looked at his mother. She had her eyes closed and one hand over her mouth. His father was as white as the stone Buddha.

"Albert didn't want anyone to know who he was. He had a new life. His brother came to find him, perhaps to seek his advice, or hide away himself, but Albert didn't want him close. The thing is, there may have been a dispute, probably about money. Albert was, it seems, still the king. Ludwig had taken the throne until things settled down – even though everyone knew they never would. So when Ludwig came to England himself, Albert would have had a right to share the crown jewels."

"And Ludwig refused?" asked Alf.

"We don't know. But I wonder whether Percival Merriweather knew something, and stole the jewels because he felt they belonged to Albert. At the same time, he could not allow anyone to know he had stolen them because that would have revealed Albert's true identity, something Albert quite clearly would not have wanted."

"But why didn't he tell us?" said Hattie. "He could have told us the whole story, we could have dug up the jewels and that would have been that."

"I'm not sure," said the professor. "But who knows? Merriweather had been tracked by a detective for a long time, and may have thought Ludwig's family could still claim the treasure."

"And the detective was hired by Ludwig," said Alf. "So Craddock was right to be careful."

"But I still don't see why he couldn't have just told us," said Hattie, impatiently.

"Perhaps telling you would have made it clear he was guilty of the crime," the professor answered. "Maybe he never thought of himself as a real criminal. If he hadn't helped himself to the other precious items in the Imperial's vault, he could have presented himself as someone who was only doing what was right. But he got greedy and stole innocent people's things too. He sold those valuables, and probably did quite well out of them."

Alf looked at his father. Hattie was studying her hands and frowning, as if working something out.

"My belief," continued the professor, "is that Percival Merriweather, in his disguise as Lord Craddock, was happy here. He was happy for the first time in his life. As Merriweather he loved Albert and later, when he returned as Lord Craddock, I think he loved you. He wasn't sure what would happen if he told you about the treasure he had buried in the garden. He tried to tell you, I think. But never quite managed it."

"But," said Hattie at last, "if Albert was the real King of Pomerania, doesn't that mean. . ."

Professor Carmichael took a step forward. "I don't know if I should get down on one knee to hand you this," she said. She held out the letter for Alf's father. "That's the proof." Then she handed him the second piece of paper. "And that's your family tree."

She looked at Tom, blinked, then bowed her head. "Your Majesty," she said.

Hattie screamed. "Dad! You're the king of Pomerania!"

213

THIRTY-FOUR

Alf stood on the steps of the Old Forge Hotel, proud and tall in his new bellboy's uniform. It was a brilliant blue, handmade, and fitted him perfectly.

It was a beautiful morning in Milton Wells, and for Alf, the best day of his life.

Soon he and Hattie would have to return to school. The attention in the press had brought the authorities to the hotel. Mr and Mrs Picton were given a stern telling off for keeping their children at home. The extraordinary circumstances, however, meant they would not be prosecuted. But from now on Alf would be a part-time bellboy only.

At any moment the mayor would be arriving and the presentation would be made. A few months ago this would have seemed impossible, but now it was about to happen.

Across the square the Imperial Hotel was surrounded by scaffolding. A decision still hadn't been made, but the outlook wasn't good. The

Imperial stood on a thin crust of rock over what cavers now called Merriweather's Chimney. It was rumoured that the hotel would have to be demolished, that it would never be safe.

With the exception of the crown, which was still in a bank vault in Wornham, the Pomeranian crown jewels had been sold at auction. Tom Picton may have been the king of Pomerania, but he was a king without a country, just as his grandfather Albert had been. Alf's parents had still not recovered from the shock. And when they were presented with the cheque of the proceeds of the auction, they were speechless. But not quite as speechless as they were when Alf owned up to concealing hundreds of letters and urgent demands for payment in the hedge.

The sodden and rotting envelopes were retrieved from their dark, damp hiding place. They were hung on pegs on a line in the kitchen, then carefully opened and read.

For at least a week Sarah Picton sat in the office writing to all the people the Old Forge Hotel owed money, explaining that their post had somehow been "misdirected". Now and again it crossed her mind to shove Alf in the hedge for all the trouble he had caused.

The gardens had been restored, and looked glorious. Every room had been redecorated, even

Craddock's. The photograph of Albert and Mary hung in there now, as did the portrait of Percival Merriweather, elegantly framed. A display cabinet was mounted on a wall. This contained Craddock's hats and cane, his pipes and, of course, the cup he won at snooker.

In the newly refurbished reception area, there was a space on the wall where the photograph of Albert and Mary had once hung. It wouldn't be empty for long.

The old ballroom had been renovated and opened for the first time in at least ten years, and was now used for conferences. This week, the Old Forge Hotel was hosting the first Cavers' and Potholers' Convention. They were full, and booked up for months to come.

The mayor's car turned the corner out of North Parade and into the square. Alf ran in and yelled, "He's here! Come on! He's here!"

Alf's mother, father and sister, Purvis and Cardew, his arm and leg now out of plaster, gathered behind the bellboy. Max and Tilda, no longer guests, but employed by Mr and Mrs Picton to run the hotel's new conference facilities, stood at one end, the professor at the other. The photographer, who had been waiting contently in the garden, stepped out last.

The mayor leapt out of the back of the big

glossy black car. He was a little man with a bald head and a tiny moustache. He climbed up the few steps and stood next to the bellboy.

The photographer positioned himself on the pavement.

"I will keep this brief," said the mayor. "It is my great privilege to be here this afternoon. The Chamber of Trade and Commerce is obliged by council decree to present this cup to the hotel that has brought the most business and tourism to our beloved town. So, for the first time in sixty years, the Old Forge is Milton Wells' Hotel of the Year."

He passed Alf the cup and shook his hand.

"Congratulations, all of you," he said.

The photographer ordered everyone to smile, and they did.

Look out for this. . .

He didn't ask to be famous!

OSWALD
AND THE END OF
THE WORLD

ANDREW STRONG